Twins Write 2 | Lakisha Johnson

Gratitude

God, I thank you. It is because of your anointing that I am able to do what I love. When you should have given up on me, you gave me mercy instead. When you should have forgotten me, you favored me instead. THANK YOU!

To my amazing husband, my Gabrielle and my CJ; who willingly share me with the world … I love y'all and thank you.

My twin sister/bestfran, LaQuisha. If I call, she's coming, no questions asked. Sister, I cannot wait to add you to the payroll. (Come on God!)

To each of you, who continually support me, I'd never be able to thank you enough. It is because of you that I enjoy writing. Please don't stop.

Gratitude

God: thank you. It is because of your anointing that I am able to do what I love. When you should have given up on me, you gave me mercy instead. When you should have forgotten me, you favored me instead. THANK YOU!

To my amazing husband, my Gabriela and my OJ, who willingly share me with the world ... I love y'all and thank you.

My twin sister/bestian, LaQuiane. If I call, she's coming, no questions asked. Sister, I cannot wait to add you to the payroll. (Come on God!)

To each of you, who continually support me, I'll never be able to thank you enough. It is because of you that I enjoy writing. Please, don't stop.

Dedication

This book is dedicated to YOU. Never give up on your dreams, no matter how hard it gets.

After the broken hearts, crushed promises and shattered trust, caused by sin and fleshly lust; came pain, forgiveness and the chance to start over. But is it too late for some marriages to recover?

When the Vows Break 3

Recovery and Restoration

Chapter 1

Chloe

"How are you feeling?" the nurse inquires when she and another nurse walks in.

"I feel fine, other than a slight headache. Is everything okay?"

"Your blood pressure is a little high, so Dr. Lane wants to run a few more tests. We're going to get some blood and urine. I'm also going to put you on a catheter and a heart monitor, for the baby because Dr. Lane doesn't want you getting up."

One of them gets blood while the other explains the procedure, for the catheter. When they're done, I lay back and close my eyes while the monitor is attached. When I hear the baby's heartbeat, I breathe a sigh of relief.

"We're done," she tells me, "and I'll be back later but if you need anything, press the call button."

"Thank you."

I look at the door and Todd still hasn't come back, so I turn out the light, over the bed and roll on my side; as best I can.

"Be good, sweet one. You need a little more time,"

I say rubbing my stomach and yawning.

Sometime later, I feel Todd get in the bed with me and I don't fight, when he wraps his arms around me. I exhale.

"Dude, what the hell are you doing?"

I turn at the sound of Todd's voice to see Chris in bed with me.

"Chris, get up," I yell, elbowing him in the chest.

He laughs. "What, a man can't lay with his wife?"

"I'm not your wife."

"Then maybe you should have removed me as your emergency contact."

"Dude, I've been here over three hours, so even if you were still my husband, you wouldn't be welcomed."

"I was busy," he shrugs.

"And you thought bringing your ass in here, climbing into my bed was the best choice."

"Well, you're sexy when you aren't talking," he smirks.

"Chris, get the hell out of here and I'll be sure to update my paperwork."

"Ah, you want to be tough in front of this pretty boy. He must be that baby's pappy?"

"Chris—ah," I cry out.

"What's wrong?" Todd asks running to me.

"My head, ah."

"Nurse! Nurse!"

"I need to ask you all to step out," she demands, coming in with two other nurses.

"Can you tell me what's going on?" Todd asks, without releasing my hand.

"We will, as soon as we get her stable. Now, please let us work."

I have my eyes closed but I hear Todd saying, he'll be right outside the door.

"Chloe, my name is Melinda. I know you're in pain, but I need you to breathe. Come on, you can do it."

"My head," I cry.

"I know but calm down as best you can."

"What happened?" I hear Dr. Lane asks.

"Her pressure spiked."

"Dr. Lane, my head is killing me," I tell him.

"Give her 10mgs of Nifedipine and another dose of the corticosteroids. Chloe, listen to me. Your pain is coming from a rise in your blood pressure. I'm going to try another medication to see if we can get it lowered, but if it doesn't work, we'll have to perform an emergency c-section."

I cry.

"I'm going to do everything I can to make sure you and baby are safe. Okay?"

I shake my head.

"Good, now try and rest. Melinda will monitor you, over the next few hours and I'll be back."

"Chloe, I'm going to turn out these lights and allow you to rest. Would you like me to send your visitors home?"

I shake my head, no. "Not Todd."

"Okay, I'll send him in but if your pressure doesn't go down, he'll have to leave. Okay?"

I nod.

"Wait, can you add him as my emergency contact? He'll give you his information but he's the one—"

"I'll take care of it."

When she leaves, a few seconds later I hear Chris yelling in the hall.

"Chloe, I'm here." Todd says, grabbing my hand. "I'm right here and I've taken care of the paperwork."

"Dr. Lane says, if they can't get my pressure down, he'll have to deliver the baby, but it's too soon."

"Shh," he rubs my forehead. "Whatever God's will is, it'll prevail."

"Can you please get my phone and call one of the girls to let them know what's happening? Whichever one you get too first, and she'll tell everybody else. My lock code is 7729."

"I will but first, let us pray." He squeezes my hand and places the other on my stomach.

"Heavenly Father, God, I thank you for the life of Chloe and our baby. God, I know I haven't always acted accordingly, forgive me. Forgive me of any sins and remove anything, within me, that can hinder this prayer. For God, I need you to saturate this room with your sweet spirit. God, you know what the doctor says yet we're trusting you.

Cover and protect Chloe and this blessing, growing within her. God, you have the ability to turn things around and while, we want this little one to remain inside, if she should come early, then we'll count it as your will being done. But, if she has to come early, then you take care of her. Strengthen lungs, heart, brain activity, veins, vessels, organs and limbs.

Do it now, God because you have the power. Not by our might but by yours. Thank you, Father, in advance. Bless the hands of Dr. Lane and his staff. Give them sound wisdom to see and understand, in order to make the right decisions. Thank you God and I humbly submit this prayer, by faith. Amen."

"Amen," I whisper before drifting to sleep.

Kerri

"Did you ever think about suicide?"

"To be honest with you, yes. While I was tricking my mind into believing, as long as I drank, I wouldn't have to deal with my problems but then, I realized, those same problems will be there when I sobered up. So, yeah, I've thought about suicide, but I could never go through with it.

Nevertheless, some people have, because they feel suicide is their only way out. And there's a misconception that suicide is easy but that's the farthest from the truth. Suicide is the hardest thing, for anybody, because to them it's their last option.

They've tried the talking, the therapy or the drugs and they've tried to be strong enough to pull themselves out but when they can't, and they no longer want to be a burden; they'll choose suicide. Others may not have tried to commit suicide but when you want the thoughts in your head to silence themselves, you will do just about anything."

I looked at him as the tears fall. "I didn't know it was that bad. How were you able to survive?"

"This is going to sound cliché, but it was only by the grace of God. One night, I'd gotten so drunk that I was in the alley of this bar, trying to use the bathroom. I don't know how I ended up there, but that's where I was. Anyway, when I finished and turned around, there was a gun in my face.

The dude, a young kid, wanted everything I had. At first, I didn't comprehend what was happening until he pressed that gun to the middle of my forehead. You talk about sobering up, quick. I'd foolishly left my wallet, keys and phone on the bar. He got so angry that he pulled the trigger, but it jammed.

It was then, as my life was flashing before—" he stops when he gets emotional, "my life was flashing before my eyes that I saw you and MJ. God allowed me to feel the pain of what you'd feel, being notified of my murder. Kerri, that dude pulled that trigger, three more times and each time, the gun didn't shoot."

He gets up from the table.

"Man, you talk about scared. It was that moment; I knew I had to get back to y'all. So, I made up my mind to do it and I did."

"Why didn't you tell me?"

"You would have offered me pity and I didn't need

pity, I had to have a plan. The plan was rehab and getting my family back. Kerri, I went to rehab and now I'm back to fight for you."

He kneels beside the table. "Kerri Janeen Davis, will you marry me again?"

Tears spill from my eyes.

"Baby, please say something."

"First," I sniff, "there's something I have to tell you." I swallow hard. "I slept with Brian."

"Brian who? Shelby's Brian? Is this a joke? This is a joke, right?"

"Michael, let me explain," I say getting up. "Brian and I met during junior high school and we dated, for a few months before him and his family moved to Knoxville. On our last date, we slept together but we were children."

"Okay, so why are you telling me this now? Is there something going on between you two, presently?"

"God no! We've never had any kind of romantic interaction or anything since then. As a matter of fact, I hadn't seen Brian in years before him and Shelby started dating. I'm only telling you this, now, because Shelby found out tonight and I didn't want you to be blindsided by it."

"If Shelby didn't know, why is this coming up now? Kerri, baby, get to the point."

"A few months back, Brian confided in me that he'd been diagnosed with cancer."

"Brian has cancer?"

I nod.

"Damn. Okay and?"

"He told me before he told Shelby but, in my defense, I begged him to tell her and he did, a while later. Tonight, when she told us about the cancer being treatable, I opened my big mouth and let it slip that I knew."

"And because you let it slip, you had to explain why Brian was comfortable telling you and not his wife?"

"Basically, and now Shelby is pissed at me."

"I can't blame her. Wouldn't you be mad to find out I was comfortable confiding in one of your friends, about my issues and not you?"

"Yea but —"

"Kerri, do you love me?"

"Yes."

"Do you want this marriage?"

"Yes."

"Is there anything going on between you and

Brian?"

"Hell no."

"Then I can't help what happened twenty years ago. I appreciate you telling me but right now, I'm trying to get my good thang back and I can't do that talking about Brian and Shelby." He kneels again. "Kerri Janeen Davis, will you marry me again?"

"Yes," I answer, throwing my arms around his neck and kissing him.

"I've missed you," he says.

"Show me."

He sits me on the kitchen counter and my phone rings, at the same time.

"Let it go to voicemail, please," he begs when it rings again.

I pause but then agree.

Ray

Getting home, I walk in to find Rashida on the couch and the boys stretched out on the floor.

"Hey, what are you doing home?" she questions.

"Chloe got sick and has to stay overnight in the hospital. She's going to be okay, but it ended our girl's night. What are y'all watching?"

"It's a movie that Sis. Renee, from church, told us to watch. It's called The Grace Card."

"What's it about?" I ask, sitting next to her.

"A man loses his son and he's filled with anger and bitterness. He's a police officer so he gets paired with another officer, named Sam, who is also a pastor."

"The dad is mad at the world but he's also mad at God but he's learning that life can change, fast."

"But," Tristan cuts in, "we have a chance to rebuild relationships by extending grace."

"Mom," JJ says sitting up. "I know we're all mad at daddy, but I think it's time we all talked. I don't know how our relationship will be, going forward but he deserves grace too."

Before I can stop myself. I have tears pouring down

my face. Rashida touches my hand.

"Are you okay?" she asks.

"Yea, I'll be right back."

I get up and walk into my bathroom. Closing the door, I lean against the sink.

"God, I need you because I'm so angry. God, how can I tell my children to extend grace, when I don't know if I can? This man, my husband, hurt me deeply. Father, please help me."

"Mom, are you okay?" Rashida asks, tapping on the door.

"Yeah, give me a minute."

Walking back into the living room, there's a song playing. I stop when I hear the lyrics.

"This is where the healing begins, oh this is where the healing starts. When you come to where you're broken within, the light meets the dark. The light meets the dark. Afraid to let your secrets out. Everything that you hid can come crashing through the door now, but you're too scared to face all your fears. So, you hide but you find that the shame won't disappear. Let it fall down. There's freedom waiting in the sound. When you let your walls fall to the ground."

"Mom, mom—"

"Huh? What?"

"You don't have to front with us," Tristan says taking my hand when I hadn't realized he was standing in front of me.

"Yea, we know how much this suck," JJ adds, "but you can cry, in front of us and we'd still know you're strong."

"It's okay," Rashida says, "we got you."

With those last words, I break and fall into the floor.

"Oh God," I scream out.

They all surround me, and I can feel their bodies trembling from their own tears.

"God, by your power," I say, rocking back and forth. "God, by your power because we can't do this alone. God, cover and protect my children then heal us, oh God and strengthen us to extend grace. Give us a heart to forgive and lips that speak love.

Don't let our flesh fight against what we don't understand but let our spirit speak to those things, you allow. For this isn't our battle. Thank you, God for never leaving us and thank you for letting us see you, even by way of a movie. We need you God and we'll continually seek you. Amen."

I wrap my arms, around them, until they are no

longer crying.

After a few minutes, they sit up.

"Thank you," I tell them. "Thank you for being my strength."

"We're strong because it's all we've ever seen of you," Rashida tells me. "I love you."

"I love you too."

We all stand, and I pull them into a hug.

JJ kisses me on the cheek before grabbing his phone and going into his room. Tristan does the same, but Rashida goes over to the couch.

She grabs the remote and turns off the TV.

"Mom," she stops and looks at me with a look of worry. "I love daddy, but I'm not ready to accept his lifestyle."

"Rashida, I will never make you do something you're not ready for. You have to make the choice on how you handle this because it can't be for me. All I ask is for you to be respectful with every decision and don't mistreat him."

"I won't, if you promise to do the same," she smiles.

"I promise."

When she leaves, my phone rings. Getting it, I slide it open and put it on speaker.

"Chloe?"

"Ray, hey, it's Todd."

"Todd, is everything okay with Chloe?"

"Her blood pressure is still high and they're trying a new medication but if it doesn't come down, in the next few hours, they'll do an emergency c-section."

"Oh no, how is she?"

"She's resting but scared."

"I'll be there. Have you called anybody else?"

"No, I tried Kerri, but she didn't answer. She said I only needed to call one of you."

"Thanks Todd, I'll take care of it and will see you soon."

Cam

Since our girl's night ended early and I wasn't ready to go home, I drive around, for a while. I pull into the parking lot of Chicks and Cigars, a new cigar bar.

I sit, for a minute trying to decide if I want to go inside or find something more interesting to get inside of me. I have to laugh at my own thoughts.

Opening my contacts, I scroll to one name and then another until I hear the girl's voices in my head saying, "Cam, take your ass home."

"Forget y'all," I say out loud, turning off the car, grabbing my purse, phone and getting out.

Walking inside, there is a live band and a fairly nice size crowd. I go into the humidor room to find a cigar. Cigar smoking isn't something I do, regularly but I've enjoyed it ever since Judge Alton, turned me on to it. There's nothing like having a good cigar and drink to mellow you out.

After finding my cigar, of choice, I make my way to the end of the bar.

"What can I get you?" the bartender asks, stopping when she recognizes me. "C," she sings, "girl, where have you been?"

"Paige, oh my God," I reach over the bar to give her a hug. "I've been busy, and I guess that's why I didn't know you were back in Memphis."

"I'm surprised Charles didn't tell you, I've been back about six months, now. Anyway, we'll have to catch up. What are you having? Your usual?"

"Hennessy Black with ginger ale," I tell her as she hands me a cutter, torch lighter and ashtray; rubbing on my hand as she sits them in front of me.

"Is this seat taken?"

I smile when I look up to see Charles or rather, Judge Alton standing there.

"Judge, fancy meeting you here."

"Camille, I thought that was you. How are you?" he questions giving me a hug. "I've missed seeing you at the courthouse."

"I'm good and I'll be back and giving you hell, in no time. How have things been?"

"You know, the same. With the crime, in Memphis, there is never a dull moment."

"Are you here alone?" I inquire.

"No, I'm with some friends. Would you like to join us?"

"No thanks. I'm not staying long."

"Well, if you change your mind, we're over in the corner. It was really good to see you."

"You too, Judge."

I watch him walk away before licking my lips. Paige sits my drink down as my phone vibrates with a text from Thomas.

THOMAS: Where are you?

ME: Hello to you too. I'm at Chicks and Cigars. Would you like to join me?

THOMAS: Wow, I'm surprised you didn't lie again.

ME: Again?

THOMAS: I thought you were at Chloe's for a "girl's night."

I roll my eyes at his use of quotations around girl's night.

ME: How did you know I wasn't?

THOMAS: I drove by and didn't see any cars.

ME: WOW! First, I don't need you checking on me. I'm not a child. Second, Chloe got sick and is staying overnight in the hospital. Third, I'M MFKIN GROWN!

THOMAS: I'm aware but I also know what grown Camille does.

"I'm not about to do this." I mouth to myself, putting

my phone on do not disturb and over into my purse.

For the next hour, I smoke my cigar and enjoy the music and drinks. I pay my tab and head to the bathroom. When I'm done, I walk out but is pulled into a dark corner.

A warm mouth covers mine.

"Hmm. Did you really think I'd let you leave without tasting you?"

I smile. "I'm flattered but I can't, not tonight," I tell her.

"Come on C, you know it's been a while."

"I know babe, but I've got to get home."

She whines.

"I'll make it up to you, next time."

I silently curse myself for turning that licking down but I'm tired. Fifteen minutes later, I'm home. I turn the alarm off and back on before heading to the guest room, where I'm still staying. Coming out of the bathroom, after a shower, I jump at Thomas sitting there.

"I'm surprised you came home," he sarcastically says. "I thought you'd be somewhere sleeping with somebody else's husband or wife, for that matter because that's what the great Camille Shannon does."

"Are you drunk?" I inquire.

"Are you?"

"Thomas, I am not in the mood to entertain your insecurities. I'm tired and going to bed. Please close the door behind you, on the way out."

"Did you sleep with someone tonight?"

"Really?" I laugh. "No but to be honest, I wanted too. You know why? Because it's been months, since my husband or anybody has touched me. I told you, I was working on me, and I am. That's why, when I was propositioned tonight, I turned it down.

Only to come home, to this freaking guest room and horny as hell. Oh, but the next time, I'll go on and cheat since you're going to accuse me, anyway."

"Why am I not enough for you?"

"Thomas, please leave."

"I miss you," he blurts. "I miss you, but I don't trust you."

"If you miss me, then say that but I will not continue to apologize for the past. I messed up and you don't trust me. I KNOW," I yell, "I know because you won't let me forget."

"I'm trying."

"No, you're not because if you were trying, we'd be

working together to fix our marriage. What you're doing is trying to control me. Thomas, I'm sorry I hurt you, but I can't make you trust me and if we're going to argue, each time I leave here; then maybe it's time I find my own place."

"Damn it, Camille," he says, moving quickly to kiss me. He backs me into the wall and kisses me, so passionately that I'm scared to move. "I've missed you." He kisses my neck, down to my chest then my breast.

I push him back. "Wait, are you sure this is what you want because I—"

He smacks my hand away, snatches my gown over my head and kicks my legs open.

"At this very moment, I want my wife. We'll deal with everything else, tomorrow."

With that, I slide his pajama pants down and wrap my hands around his neck. He picks me up, carrying me over to the bed where he lays me at the edge.

"Oh," I moan as he moves to the one spot, he knows all too well. It doesn't take long before he's entering me. I open my eyes to find him looking at me. I pull him closer, wrapping my legs around him as our lips touch.

When we're done, he grabs his pajama pants and leave out the room. I get up and get my gown when my phone rings with a call from Ray.

Lyn

I begin to cry, hitting the floor. When I see the pills, I crawl over to where they are, picking two more but then, I remember throwing the water.

The song, next door replays. I get up and go into the kitchen, putting the pills into my mouth. Turning on the water, in the sink, I cup my hand under it and sip the water.

I try to swallow but the pills will not go down. I get more water but still, the pills feel like they have tripled in size. I try more water but the same thing.

I spit them in the sink.

"What do you want from me?" I scream, sliding down into the floor.

More music plays.

"Show me your face, fill up this space. My world needs you right now. My world needs you right now. I can't escape, being afraid. Fill me with you right now. My world needs you right now"

"Please stop," I cry. "Please stop."

"Power fall down, bring with it a sound that points us to you right now. Erase substitutes right now, fix *what I see, and God please fix me. My world needs you right now. Let us see you right now."*

I jump up and grab my purse, but it falls. When it hits the floor, the only thing that comes out is a card. I pick it up.

Chaplain Denise French.

I grab it, along with my purse and bolt for the door. A little bit later, I'm sitting in my truck, in a half empty parking lot. I keep turning the card over in my hand until finally, I let out a breath and dial the number.

"Hello, this is Denise French."

"Chaplain French, you may not remember me, but I need your help."

"Lynesha Williams," she cuts in. "I knew you'd call."

"How, how did you know?"

"You asked God a question, didn't you? My address is 9632 Pilgrim Way, Olive Branch, MS. I'll be waiting for you. 9632 Pilgrim Way, Olive Branch, MS;" she repeats before hanging up."

I quickly input the address into the GPS and put my truck into drive before I talk myself out of it. Thirty minutes later, I pull up to a house, that looks more like a farm. I'm still sitting in my truck, when the light, on the front porch, comes on.

Sighing, I get out and walk up the driveway. She's standing in the foyer, of the house, when I walk in.

"You were trying to talk yourself out of coming in, weren't you?"

I nod.

"I'm glad you didn't. Come on in. You can leave your things there and follow me. I have some water and wine, set up in my living room."

"You drink wine?"

"Child, yes. Ain't nothing wrong with a little wine to knock the edge off and it's good for your stomach. That's bible," she laughs. "Before you sit, let us have a word of prayer."

I grab her hand.

"Dear God, thank you for your matchless grace, you so abundantly give and thank you for allowing us to gather, in this safe place. Now God, allow the sweet communion of your spirit to abide with us as we seek to find peace and understanding. Bless me, oh Lord, that I might do your will and not mine. Amen."

"Amen," I say.

"Help yourself to a drink or you can wait."

"I'll wait."

"Very well. Why are you here Lynesha?"

"I feel like I'm losing my mind. A few months ago, I was raped. Now, every time I close my eyes, I feel that man on top of me with his hand around my throat. I hear his voice, in my ear and nothing I do can stop it. On top of that, on the same day, I found out my husband has been having an affair, for over three years."

"You're angry?"

"Damn—I mean, yes. Don't I have a right to be?"

"Lynesha—"

"Please call me Lyn."

"Lyn, you have every right to be angry."

"Oh, I am, trust me. I feel like, if I don't get control of this, I'm going to hurt somebody."

My leg is shaking and I'm constantly squeezing my hands together.

"Have you ever heard of PTSD?"

"The thing that soldiers get?"

"Yes," she replies, "but it's not just soldiers. PTSD is a disorder that causes a person to have difficulty getting over a traumatic event. Lyn, you faced two in one day and it's not uncommon for you to experience anger."

"It's not so much the rape or Paul's infidelity. The

thing that angers me the most is Paul not being there when I needed him. He chose his baby's mother, over me."

"So, had he been there, you'd forgive him?"

I look at her.

"If your husband would have been there, to stop the assault, you'd forgive him for cheating?" she asks again.

"I don't know," I scream. "I don't know anything, anymore. I just want this pain to stop."

She comes over and sits beside me. I have my arms wrapped at my waist and I'm rocking, back and forth.

"Lyn, give your pain a voice. When you're in pain and you go to the doctor, in order to get help, you have to first tell him or her what the problem is and then try the remedy, they suggest. Give your pain a voice. What are you angry about?"

"The rape," I say as tears begin to sting my eyes.

"What else?"

"My husband cheated and had a baby."

"What else?"

"My daughter knew."

"What else?"

"I want to hurt myself." With the last sentence, I scream. Over and over, I scream, and she allows me too. When I finally calm down, she stands.

"Come with me, Lyn."

I follow her through the house and out onto her back porch.

"Should I get my jacket?"

"No, you won't need it. You're about a nine, in shoes, right?"

"Yes ma'am," I reply with confusion.

"Put these on," she says handing me some boots.

Once we've changed shoes, I follow her down a path. We come to a clearing, take a left and go up a hill. Once on top, there's another, larger shed that's painted red.

"Wow. Your property is beautiful."

She smiles, pushes open the door and the inside look even better than outside. There are huge letters on the wall, spelling, 'Get It Out," and there are different areas.

"I call this area, my get it out, space. Here, in this sacred place, is where I come to get out my frustrations because holding it in, gives a foot hole to the enemy and baby, we ain't got time for that," she laughs. "Lyn, when you have a toothache, headache or sickness; do you stay in pain or do something about it?"

"Do something about it."

"Yes, because you know, or you hope, it can help with the pain. Well, think about the physical and mental pain, you're experiencing. In order to get help, you have to first acknowledge there's a problem. Tonight, you asked God a question, didn't you?"

"How—never mind, yes. I asked Him, what He wants from me."

"Well, He told me to tell you, He wants you restored."

I chuckle. "As do I, but that's easier said than done." I say, walking over to an area and picking up an old picture frame.

"It is but it can be done. If this is truly what you want."

"If this is what I want? I didn't ask for this. I didn't ask for my husband to cheat or for a monster to rape me. I didn't ask for these freaking nightmares," I yell, throwing the frame. "Now, I guess I'm supposed to be happy that God wants me restored when He's the one who allowed me to be broken, in the first place. Should I shave my head, tear my clothes and sit in an ash pile like Job, too?"

"Lyn, baby, you aren't Job," she calmly tells me, "and even if you were as blameless as he was, you aren't exempt from trouble and you doggone sure, don't have to ask for it. Look, shit happens."

I look at her and she shrugs.

"I said what I said, and I will not apologize for my bluntness because it's true. Nobody asks for trouble, including Job, yet it happens, and we can either die in it or survive. Lyn, I know you're angry because of all the things, God has allowed to transpire in your life but hurting others or yourself, will not solve that."

"YOU DON'T KNOW! NOBODY KNOWS! Nobody knows what the hell is happening with me because I don't. All I'm sure of, I'm tired."

"Lyn—"

"No," I tell her, putting up my hands. "I can't do this." I leave out of the shed and run back, the way we came. I don't even stop to change shoes. Instead, I go inside and grab my stuff.

Getting inside my truck, I drive until I see a sign.

Memphis International Airport.

Shelby

"Can you please stop that music?" I scream.

He presses mute on the remote.

"I messed up Shelby and I'm sorry. I never meant to hurt you."

"What else is there?"

"What do you mean?" he questions.

"What other secrets are you keeping? Do I have to worry about being blindsided by anything else that my husband should have told me? Is there anything else you've confided to Kerri or anybody else?"

"No, baby. I promise."

"Is there something going on between you and her?"

"No, God no."

"I wish I could believe you, but I don't."

"Baby, please wait," he says when I turn to leave.

"Brian, I appreciate the effort you put into this but right now, I'm not in the mood to sit in the midst of a sand box with you, after hugging this out and forgetting it, neither am I in the mood to forgive.

Especially knowing, one of my best friends is who

you ran too when you were scared and not me." I state. "Oh, I also know that y'all took each other's virginity. Imagine how that must have been, to find out in front of all the girls. Good night Brian."

I go upstairs to undress and shower when I hear a loud crash. I run back down, to see Brian in the middle of the floor having a seizure.

"Oh my God," I yell, rushing to him. "Brian," I turn him on his side before getting up to get his phone off the mantle.

"911, what's your emergency?"

"My husband is having a seizure. The address is 1024 Galaxy Trail. Please hurry. Brian, baby, hold on."

*****

"Dr. Harper," I sprout up from my chair. "How is he?"

"He's stable," he replies guiding me to the chair, "but he had another seizure."

"Oh my God."

"Shelby, the seizures aren't uncommon, with this type of cancer. Brian has been fortunate enough to not have them, up until now. However, he's stable. I'm going to have another MRI, done tonight but if my assumptions are correct, the tumor has increased in size."

"What do we do?"

"Unfortunately, we're going to have to move ahead with the surgery."

"When?"

"First thing in the morning. I've started him on antibiotics and anti-seizure medicines, in preparation. After the MRI, he'll be moved to the surgical floor."

"Is he awake? Can I see him?"

"Yes, but he's had some medication to bring him out of the seizure, so he may be in and out. Follow me."

"Thank you, Dr. Harper."

Getting to the door, Brian is lying in the bed with his eyes closed.

"Brian."

He opens his eyes and holds out his hand.

"Babe—"

"Shh," I say, climbing into the bed with him.

"Shelby, I'm sorry for not telling you about Kerri. I was foolish and handled this entire situation wrong, but you have to know, there's nothing going on between us. I just, I messed everything up and I'm sorry. If something would have happened—"

I feel his tears hitting my face and that makes me cry.

"I'm so sorry," he says.

After a few minutes of both of us crying, I raise up, wiping his face before kissing him.

"Shelby, I'm so sorry."

"I know but let me explain something and then we will put this to rest in order to get you well." I sit up on the side of the bed, wiping the tears from my face. "I can't be upset that you knew her first but finding out about it tonight, pissed me off because it was yet another secret. Then I get home and you'd gone through so much, to make the night special and I couldn't see pass the hurt for not being the one you ran too," I pause, "but I can't change that."

I stand up as tears continue to fall. "Brian, I love you and I cannot imagine my life without you. Seeing you tonight, helpless, made me realize that life is too short to hold grudges. Yes, I'm mad at you but tonight, at 11:22 PM, we make a vow to forgive each other, for anything that happened before now, and we move ahead. As long as there are no more secrets."

"There aren't, I promise, and I'll spend the rest of my life making sure you know, just how much I appreciate you."

"No, let's spend the rest of our lives, making the best of another opportunity God has given us. Okay?"

"Okay," he smiles before pulling me to him to kiss me. I deepen the kiss.

"If you keep this up, I'm going to forget I'm in this hospital bed."

"Boy," I laugh, slapping his arm. "You just had some this morning and besides that, you've had two seizures, not even an hour ago."

"I know but whatever medicine Dr. Harper gave me, has me feeling really good," he laughs, "and I feel like I can go all night."

"Yea, well keep that same energy when you get home."

He laughs, again. "I love you Mrs. James and I'm sorry that we'll be spending Christmas, with me recovering."

"As long as we're together and you're alive, that's all that matters, and I love you, too."

"Mr. James?"

We both look up to see a young man, standing in the door.

"My name is Neil and I'm here to take you down for

an MRI. He may have a room assigned, by the time we're done but the nurse can let you know."

"I'll see you when you're done," I say kissing him again. When they wheel him out, I grab my phone and sit in the chair, in the corner. I see a few missed calls from Ray, but I decide to call Mrs. Gray, first to give her an update.

Next, I dial Ray's number and she tells me that she's upstairs, in labor and delivery with Chloe. I leave my cell phone number, with the nurse, so she can let me know what room Brian will be moved too.

Getting to Chloe's room, Ray and Todd are sitting next to the bed.

"Hey," I whisper, "how is she?"

She stands up and we walk to the door.

"Her blood pressure is still a little high, but Dr. Lane is waiting to see, if it goes down anymore. If it doesn't, within the hour, he's going to deliver the baby."

"I know she is terrified."

"Yea, but she's asleep now and Todd called his mom, who is coming to pray. How is Brian and why didn't you call me, sooner?"

"Ray, stuff happened so fast that I wasn't even thinking. I felt so bad because one minute he's standing there, in the middle of a sandbox, trying to replicate a beach vacation and the next we're arguing about the mess with Kerri. I don't know what I would have done, had—"

"No, don't go there. You said the doctor told you, he's stable now. We will not think about what ifs. I only hope you all took the time to make up."

"We did but man, I'd be glad when this storm is over."

Just then, the machine starts beeping in Chloe's room and we hear the nurse calling Dr. Lane.

Chapter 2

Ray

"What's happening?" I ask one of the nurses, but she runs right by us as other nurses come into the room.

"Chloe, your pressure is spiking again, and we can't wait any longer," one of the nurses tell her. "I've already called Dr. Lane and he's going to meet us upstairs. Sir, we're taking her to surgery. We'll come and get you, as soon as we can."

They rush out, pass us, leaving us all standing there.

"Y'all, let's pray," Shelby says, and we all grab hands.

"Dear God, I come to you, in the midst of chaos and calamity, asking you to calm our storm. God, as we stand in the middle of this hospital room, we ask that you have your way. You know the circumstances but at this very moment, we need you to work. In the operating room, work and in the MRI department, for my husband, work. Jesus," she cries out then we hear another voice.

"God, you have the power to be everywhere and

that's where we need you. We need you to guide the hands, eyes and minds of doctors and nurses. We need you to breathe power into the baby that's about to be born early. God, you are the power and that's why we're asking you to save, tonight.

Chloe needs you God, not just for the baby but for her. God, regulate blood pressure and organ functions then give breath to the little baby. But don't just stop there, go down to the radiology department and heal a husband, who needs you. You have the power God and we're standing on that tonight.

We don't know what your plans are but we're still believing. We have no idea, what you're doing so we'll ask for strength to handle what we have to go through. Have your way, merciful God and like the young lady said, work. Work in your time and in your way. We thank you. Amen."

We say amen to Todd's mom, closing the prayer before she gives each of us a hug.

"Shelby and Ray, this is my mother Denise and my sister Taya."

"We've met your mother before," I say before giving each of them a hug, "and Taya, it's nice to meet you."

"Rev. French, it's great to see you again," Shelby tells her, "I just wish it wasn't under these circumstances."

"I know but we have to believe that God is going to work it all out. How's your husband?" she questions.

"He has brain cancer and his doctor think the tumor is growing which caused him to have two seizures tonight. They're running some tests in preparation for surgery, in the morning."

"How is Chloe," Taya asks.

"We don't know. They rushed her into surgery and we're waiting for an update." Todd says, pacing. "Lord, let them be okay."

"They're going to be okay," his sister tells him. "Can I get anybody anything?"

We all shake our heads no.

"Mr. French," the nurse says coming in. "Your wife is in surgery now. Dr. Lane will be out to speak to you as soon as he's done."

"Thank you," Todd tells her.

Forty-five minutes later.

"Mr. French, hi, I'm Dr. Lane. Chloe made it through surgery and we delivered your baby girl."

"How are they?"

"Chloe is in recovery and doing great. The baby weighs two pounds and six ounces and is being transferred to the NICU. She's having a little trouble breathing, but she's very feisty," he laughs. "Chloe will spend some time in recovery and then moved to a room. It's going to be about an hour before you can see her, but I can have a nurse take you to the NICU to meet your daughter, if you'd like."

"Yes, please," Todd beams.

"Right this way."

"You all go ahead," Shelby says. "I'm going to check on Brian."

"I'll go with you," I tell her.

Walking to the elevator, her phone rings. When she hangs up, she looks stunned.

"Shelby, what's wrong?"

"I—I don't know but the nurse says I need to come downstairs."

"Calm down, it's probably just the doctor wanting to give you Brian's latest test results."

I take her hand. "You're shaking," I tell her.

"I'm scared. Something is not right," she says shaking her head as we get into the elevator.

When the elevator finally opens, Shelby is almost

running to the nurse's station.

"Shelby," a doctor says meeting us and she stops in her tracks.

"Dr. Harper, what happened?"

"Let's go in here and talk," he says grabbing her arm and I follow them into an empty room.

"Did you find something else on Brian's MRI?"

"Please sit down," he motions for her and she does. I stand behind her.

"Just say it," Shelby says.

"While Brian was getting the MRI, he had another seizure. He was inside the machine and hit his head."

"Okay but he's alright, right? You said seizures are common with this type of cancer."

"They are but Shelby," he pauses, "his head injury was severe, and we worked for over thirty minutes to revive him, but we were unsuccessful. Brian, didn't survive Shelby and I'm so sorry."

My hand flies to my mouth and she stares at him without saying anything.

"Shelby—"

"No, you're wrong. Where is he?"

"Shelby, Brian is gone."

"WHERE IS HE?" she screams. "Where is my

husband?"

I grab her, but she snatches away and stands up.

"Dr. Harper, take me to my husband, please."

He stands, and we walk behind him. I try to grab Shelby's hand, but she snatches away. Getting to a door, Dr. Harper pauses with his hand on the knob.

Turning it, the door slowly opens, and we see Brian laying on the bed, a sheet up to his neck. Shelby rushes over to him.

"Brian, baby, I'm right here. Brian, please wake up. I'm here. Brian, please! Please baby, wake up."

She's shaking him, screaming.

"Ray!" she screams. "Tell them to do something, please Ray. Tell them to save my husband."

I go over to her as she lays her head on his chest, screaming.

"He's gone, sister. Brian is gone."

"Oh God, no. Noooooo." She lets out a blood curdling cry. Dr. Harper calls for a nurse to bring something, to give her. They move her to the empty bed.

"You all will either need to move him or her because she cannot see him when she wakes up."

Cam

"Ray, what's wrong? Is it Chloe? What happened?" she asks, running into the room. "Wait, that's not Chloe."

I can barely get it out, "Brian is gone."

"Gone? Gone where?"

She gets up and pulls me into the hall.

"Ray, what the hell happened?"

"He had a seizure and hit his head, they couldn't revive him," she tells me as her cell phone rings. "This is Kerri, can you—" she hands me the phone and walks off.

"Kerri."

"Hey Ray—Cam, hey, what's going on? Ray called me."

"Um," I say wiping my face. "Where are you?"

"I'm at home. What? Did something happen to Chloe?"

I shake my head and then realize she can't see me.

"Kerri, it's not Chloe. It's Shelby."

"Shelby? What happened to Shelby?"

I take a deep breath. "Brian died, tonight K."

She screams.

"Kerri, Kerri—"

"Hello, hey, it's Michael. What happened?"

"Brian is gone. He, he um, had a seizure and died. We're at Methodist Germantown, in the emergency department. Get here."

"We're on the way."

"I need to call Todd. He's upstairs with Chloe." Ray says, walking back over.

I hand her back her phone and press my back against the wall to call Thomas.

Hanging up, I hear Shelby crying. I motion for Ray and we go back inside.

"Shelby, we're right here."

"He's gone. Brian is gone," she cries.

"I know, and I am so sorry. Is there anything you need me to do?"

"Can someone please call Ms. Gray? She has the baby."

"I'll call her. What else?"

"I don't know. I don't know."

"Shelby," Dr. Harper says coming in. "There's some paperwork you'll have to fill out, to release Brian's body to the Medical Examiner."

"Medical Examiner? Why?"

"It's customary for an autopsy to be performed when a death is sudden."

"We can take care of it," Cam says.

"Wait," Shelby says. "Can I see him again? Can I see my husband?"

"Of course. Come with me and I will take you to him."

As we get ready to walk out, Kerri and Mike come in. "Cam?"

"We're going to see Brian."

We somberly walk down the hall with Ray holding on to Shelby.

We go into the room and there's a nurse standing near the bed, her face void of emotion. Who could ever get used to this?

It seems like everybody is holding their breath because there isn't a sound being made.

"Shelby, when you're ready Nurse Leann will remove the sheet," Dr. Harper says.

"I'm ready," she whispers.

Dr. Harper nods and Leann pulls the sheet back and it feels like my legs turn to jelly as I reach out to Kerri.

Shelby isn't saying anything as she walks over to him, bending down to kiss him and rub his face. "What am I supposed to do without you?" she questions, laying her head on his chest, as she sobs.

We stand back and watch our sister mourn her husband without being able to help her. What can we do? We can't take away the pain she feels.

A knock on the door, followed by Pastor Reeves coming in. We nod, at her and she goes straight to Shelby.

"Shelby, it's Pastor Reeves," she tells her, but Shelby has her head on Brian's chest and all you hear are the sounds of pain, coming from within her.

"Dear God, I ask you tonight to receive your child, into your arms. Forgive any sins he may have committed, right any wrongs, pay off any debt and receive him into thy kingdom. For he's yours and although we don't understand why death comes, when it does, we know he's only fulfilling his responsibility.

Brian is yours and we have no right to question you, for taking back what you created. Brian is in your care and we ask that you give him the healing, earth couldn't give. Then, oh God, strengthen this wife who's left behind to raise a daughter. Answer any question she may have, comfort and send peace.

Peace that will allow her to sleep, peace that will allow her to grieve but not fall into depression and peace to know that to be absent from this old body; means to be present with you. Send strength for these friends who she'll need in the days, weeks and months to come. Father, we still trust and depend on you. More than anything, we thank you for the time you've given us with Brian. May his memories forever sustain. Amen."

When she's done, Shelby gives her a hug.

"Shelby, whatever you need, we are here for you." Pastor Reeves says.

"Thank you."

"Are you okay?" Kerri asks me.

"I honestly don't know because this is so hard, and Chloe or Lyn doesn't even know yet."

"I know but we've got to stay strong for Shelby. This is only just beginning for her. She still has to go home."

"I can't even begin to imagine what she is feeling."

"Are you ready?" we hear Ray ask Shelby.

"Yea," she said kissing Brian again. "Good night husband and I'll see you again, over the sky."

Dr. Harper is waiting out in the hallway.

"Shelby," he says taking her hand. "I'm so sorry and you have my deepest condolences."

"Thank you, Dr. Harper and I know this wasn't your fault. This was God's doing and I have to be alright with that. I want to thank you for all of your help," she says, giving him a hug.

"Leann has the paperwork and Brian's belongings for you when you're ready."

"I'll take care of that," Kerri says, walking over to the nurse's station.

"Are you ready to go home?" Ray questions.

"Did anyone talk to Ms. Gray? Was she okay because I know she has to be just as devastated?"

"She's hurt, we all are but her daughter is there with her and she said you are welcome to come and stay with her for a few days." I tell her.

"What about Chloe? Have you heard anything? Oh, God, she doesn't know, does she?"

"Not yet," Ray answers. "When I last talked to Todd, she was still in recovery."

"The baby?" Cam asks.

"It's a girl. She's two pounds and six ounces but she's here."

"Wow," Shelby says, "God takes, and He gives."

Ray

We make it to Shelby's house and Anthony is here. I don't know what made me call him, but I did and although I hadn't expected him to show up, I'm so glad he did.

"Shelby, we're here," I say, waking her from the sleep she'd cried herself into.

When she opens her eyes and looks at their house, she burst into tears. "Ray, how am I supposed to live in our home without him?"

"You'll take one minute at a time and get through it. You and Brian designed this house, together and I know he'd want you to stay here and enjoy the memories you've made."

"Oh God, this is so hard," she cries. "It hurts to breathe."

I grab her hand. "Shelby, I can't begin to imagine the pain you're feeling but I'm right here with you. You can fall apart, and I'll be right here. You can scream, and cry and I'll be right here. Just don't give up."

She squeezes my hand before stretching her arms toward the dashboard and laying her head down.

"Jesus," she keeps repeating. "Lord, Jesus."

"Take all the time you need. I'm going to let the garage up and turn off the alarm."

"I don't think I turned it on, before we left."

"Okay, I'll check but if you don't want to go inside, I can take you home with me or next door to Mrs. Gray's."

"No, I need to be here but give me a second."

I get out and meet Anthony, who pulls me into a hug.

"You okay?" he asks.

I let out a deep breath.

"Tell me what you need me to do. Anything."

"Being here is doing enough. I'm going to get Shelby in the house so that she can lie down, are you staying."

"Yes, for as long as you want me too."

I go and punch the code into the garage before opening the door, to the house to see if the alarm is on. The lights are still on, so I turn back to get Shelby from the car.

"Let's go inside so you can lie down because you know once the word gets out, your phone and doorbell won't stop ringing."

"I have to tell his employees. Oh God and his brother. They aren't close, but he needs to know."

"We'll deal with all of that but right now, you need to rest."

"I need to get my car from the hospital."

"Kerri is driving it here. Don't worry."

"Thank you, Ray." She smiles.

"You don't have to thank me because you'd do the same for me, now come on."

We walk in and as soon as we make it to the door of the living room, she stops. It's then that I see the things Brian had set.

She screams.

"If I never would have said anything about Kerri. If we never would have argued—"

"No, stop! This is nobody's fault. Brian had a seizure because of the cancer that was attacking his brain. It had nothing to do with whatever y'all argued about."

"He's gone Ray," she screams, and she continues to scream until she passes out and Anthony catches her.

"Let's take her upstairs," I tell him.

We lay her in their bed and I cover her. Anthony

leaves and I sit beside her, putting my hand on hers.

"God, I can't do this alone. I need your strength and power to be what my sister needs. Strength, God. Please strengthen and comfort."

She whimpers.

"Shh, I'm right here."

Coming downstairs, Anthony is standing at the bottom waiting. I walk into his arms and finally release the tears, I'd been holding.

"You don't have to act strong with me."

I wrap my arms around him, squeezing my hands as I try to muffle my cry.

"I got you," he says rubbing my back. "You have to be strong for Shelby but not around me. I'm here for you."

We stay that way for a few more minutes.

"Thank you, for being here."

"Have you eaten anything?"

"Not since earlier but I don't have much of an appetite right now. There are so many things running through my head. I mean, look at how fast life can change. Brian went to the hospital, after having a seizure, one the doctor thought was controlled, only to have another one during an MRI. He wasn't supposed to die." I say, sitting down on the couch.

"Death is something we all have to face, yet no one knows the day or time. This is why you have to live every day as if it's your last. I can't begin to imagine what Shelby is going through."

"Me either. It's one thing to divorce your spouse, which is hard in itself, but death is final, and you have no control over when it shows up," I sigh. "There is so much stuff to take care of and I don't even know where to begin."

"Start by taking a minute to rest. The days to come will be hard enough and the last thing I need is you getting sick. Where are the kids?"

"They're at home. I haven't even called them. I'll call Justin and have him go and talk to them. I'll be right back."

I go outside to the car to get my stuff. In trying to get Shelby in the house, I left everything. Getting my phone, I dial Justin's number.

"Ray," he answers asleep, "what's wrong?"

"I'm sorry to call so late but—um, I need you to do something for me."

"Sure, what?"

"Can you go to the house because the kids are

there. I left them because Chloe is in the hospital but," I pause.

"Raylan, what's going on?"

"Justin, Brian had a seizure and hit his head."

"A seizure? Okay, but that's treatable, right?"

"Usually but not this time. They couldn't save him," I say barely above a whisper. "He's gone."

He doesn't say anything.

"Justin? Can you get to the kids? That's all I need you to do."

"Yeah, I can," he answers sounding like he's crying. "Do you want me to tell them or wait for you?"

"You can either tell them or bring them here and I will."

"Okay and Raylan, please give Shelby my condolences."

I stay outside a little while longer to call my mom. She's adamant about flying down immediately but I beg her to come after we've had a few days to make arrangements.

I send my assistant, an email, I know she'll get in a few hours, to cancel all my upcoming meetings for the next two weeks.

"Lord, we need you."

Lyn

"Well, He told me to tell you, He wants you restored."

I chuckle. "As do I, but that's easier said than done." I say, walking over to an area and picking up an old picture frame.

"It is but it can be done. If this is truly what you want."

"If this is what I want? I didn't ask for this. I didn't ask for my husband to cheat or for a monster to rape me. I didn't ask for these freaking nightmares," I yell, throwing the frame. "Now, I guess I'm supposed to be happy that God wants me restored when He's the one who allowed me to be broken, in the first place. Should I shave my head, tear my clothes and sit in an ash pile like Job, too?"

"Lyn, baby, you aren't Job," she calmly tells me, "and even if you were as blameless as he was, you aren't exempt from trouble and you doggone sure, don't have to ask for it. Look, shit happens."

I look at her and she shrugs.

"I said what I said, and I will not apologize for my

bluntness because it's true. Nobody asks for trouble, including Job, yet it happens, and we can either die in it or survive. Lyn, I know you're angry because of all the things, God has allowed to transpire in your life but hurting others or yourself, will not solve that."

"YOU DON'T KNOW! NOBODY KNOWS! Nobody knows what the hell is happening with me because I don't. All I'm sure of, I'm tired."

"This is a courtesy page for passenger Alvarez Jimenez. Please report to gate—"

I snap out of my thoughts and look around to see that I'm sitting at the gate, well a gate, at the airport. I turn the ticket over to see where I'm going because I wasn't actually paying attention when I purchased it.

Montego Bay, Jamaica. I chuckle at myself.

First, I don't even have my passport and second, no luggage yet I'm sitting here like I can really board this 5:23 AM flight.

I pull my phone out of my purse and see all the missed calls and texts from Ray, Cam and Kerri.

RAY: Lyn, where are you? Please answer the phone. Lyn, call me because it's urgent.

Kerri: Lyn, please call me.

Cam: Bitch, answer the phone or I'm driving to every apartment building downtown, until I find you.

I shake my head and dial Cam's number.

"Girl, where have you been?" she barks.

"Dealing with something. What's up? Did something happen to Chloe and the baby."

"Chloe had the baby. It's a girl, two pounds and six ounces but—"

"That's great. Are they both okay?"

"Yea, but Lyn, where are you?"

"Now boarding flight—"

"Lynesha Williams, are you at the airport?"

"Cam, I can't talk right now."

"No Lyn, wait, Brian is gone," she blurts.

"Gone where?"

"He's dead. Why do you think we've called you all these times? He died."

"Dead? How?"

"He had a seizure."

"Oh my God. Where's Shelby?"

"Ray is taking her home. I'm at the hospital with Chloe because she doesn't know yet."

I sigh.

"Lyn, I don't know what's going on but don't leave.

Not like this and not when we need each other. Please."

"Now boarding group B for flight—"

I hang up.

*****

"Lyn?" Paul asks pulling the door open. "What are you doing? It's after three, in the morning."

"Brian is dead, and I need my passport." I push pass him, but he grabs my arm.

"Wait, what did you say?"

I huff. "Brian is dead, and I need my passport."

"Brian James?"

"How many other men named Brian do you know?"

"Lyn, wait, damn! Please tell me what's going on?"

"What's going on? Life is going on Paul. FREAKING LIFE! Life that causes people to cheat and lie and life that causes people to die. That's what's going on."

I try to walk off, again but he grabs me.

"Lyn, baby, please stop. Stop running."

"I can't," I relent. "If I stop, life may just get me next."

He pulls me into a hug, but I push him away.

"No Paul, I can't do this."

"You're hurting, and you need help," he tells me.

"I don't need help, but I do need my passport."

I walk down the hall into our bedroom. I go into the closet and begin moving stuff around.

"Where are you going?"

I pull the plane ticket from my back pocket.

"Montego Bay."

"Jamaica?"

"Unless you know another Montego Bay."

"Lyn, you can't leave now. Shelby is going to need you."

"Nobody needs me."

"That's not true. Damn it, Lyn, stop. This isn't you."

"How do you know, Paul? It's apparent, neither of us knows each other, right? I mean, you have an entire new life, with a son and our daughter. What do I have, other than a scar that reminds me every day of being raped and a broken heart? What do I have?"

"Lyn, come on! How long are you going to use this as an excuse to act out? Yes, I hurt you and yes, you were attacked but it's not like people aren't surviving far worse, every day."

"Act out?" I laugh. "You think this is acting out. Acting out would have been beating the windows out your car, showing out on your job, spray painting the garage to let the neighbors know that you're a cheater. Acting out would have been setting this house on fire and not caring, if you made it out. Acting out would have been me, bashing your fucking head in.

This, what I'm doing isn't acting out. Me, wanting to end my life, isn't acting out but it's wanting the nightmares to stop. And me leaving, it isn't acting out but it's me getting away before I black out and commit murder."

He sighs. "You need help, Lyn."

"Since you know everything, tell me what kind of help I need."

"Professional help. I'll call somebody or find a program for you."

"Oh, what you mean is, you'll have unstable ass Lyn committed to some facility, so you and your baby momma can laugh, at my expense? Well, no thank you."

"That's not what I mean."

"Man, you don't know what the hell you mean. All you're good for is loose lips and lying. Well save it."

I finally find my passport.

"Goodbye, again."

I leave out and head to my apartment.

"Good morning ma'am," security says. I wave at him and walk towards the elevator but then turn back.

"Excuse me."

"Yes ma'am."

"How can I file a complaint about one of my neighbors who plays their music extremely too loud?"

He shakes the mouse to wake the computer.

"What apartment?"

"Um," I say trying to think. 706."

He taps on the keyboard. "706?" he inquires.

"Yea."

"706 shows to be unoccupied, at the moment. It's been that way for over two weeks, so I guess, you won't have to file that complaint, after all." He smiles.

"I guess not. Thank you."

Getting off the elevator, on my floor, I walk towards my door.

"He told me to tell you, He wants you restored."

I open my door and go inside. "Well, God, if you want me restored, you'll have to do it."

Kerri

"Hey, how's Shelby?" Cam asks Ray, once we walk inside.

"She's asleep, for now." I tell them. "How is Chloe?"

"I didn't tell her because she was in so much pain, already. The doctor gave her some medicine to help her rest, so she was sleeping when we left. Todd and his family are there with her and he's going to tell her, in the morning."

"Has anybody talked to Lyn because she isn't responding to anything."

"I talked to her and she was at the airport," Cam says.

"Airport? Going where?"

"I don't know, and she wouldn't say."

"Did you at least tell her about Brian and Chloe?"

"I did but she hung up," she replies. "I'm worried about her? As a matter of fact, I'm going to try and find her. She needs us, just as much as Shelby. I'll be back."

"I'm going to clean up the living room," Ray tells me.

"I'll help."

An hour later, we've removed the candles, the sandbox and all the stuff left behind; by the EMTs. We found, one of the letters, Brian had written Shelby and it caused all of us to cry.

Anthony is gone to get some food, so we're all sitting around.

"Man, life has a way of getting your attention, doesn't it?" I ask.

"That it does but Kerri, why didn't you tell Shelby about knowing Brian?"

"I don't know Ray? I guess I thought it didn't matter because we hadn't seen each other since we were fifteen."

"Maybe not but you should have told her when he came to you," Ray says.

"I know but I didn't know how. I just wish things could be different," I cry.

"Don't we all. Did you get everything taken care of at the hospital?"

"Yeah, I have the paperwork they gave me, and I put Brian's things in the laundry room."

"What funeral home did you choose?"

"Harrisons. I remembered us talking about them one day, I don't know why," I tell her, "but it's the only one I could think of."

"If it isn't right, she can change it."

"Change what?" Shelby asks, walking in.

"Hey, how are you feeling?" I ask.

"Like my husband just died. Now, change what?"

"The funeral home," I stutter. "I chose Harrisons—"

"You chose?" Shelby cuts me off. "Why are you choosing anything in relations to my husband?"

"I didn't mean it like that. I had to pick a funeral home and I remembered us talking about Harrisons before. If it isn't the one you want, I'll call them."

"No! I don't need you doing anything. As a matter of fact, get out! Ray, you too. Just leave me alone."

Neither of us moves.

"GET OUT!" she screams.

"Shelby, you can scream at us, throw things, curse and whatever else but we aren't leaving you, not like this." Ray says standing in front of her.

"Just leave me alone," she cries. "Just leave me alone."

I'm crying, and Ray holds her hand out to me.

"Shelby, I'm sorry. I know I messed up and you have every right to be mad at me. You can yell and even hit me but I'm not leaving either," I tell her standing next to Ray. "I messed up Shelby but I'm not leaving you."

She's turning around in circles. We surround her.

"We're not leaving you."

"Oh my God," she says falling into the floor. "Why did God have to take him? Why?"

We both kneel as she rocks and cries.

"God, we need you," I cry. "We need you at this very moment to saturate this place with your comforting grace. God, we want to question you but instead, we'll cry out for your mercy. Have mercy on us, God. Wrap your arms around us so that we may stand, in the midst of grief and pain. Rock us, Father, when it seems like we will not make it. Guide us, so that we feel you in everything. Please God, hear my prayer, not just for me but for my sisters. We need you. Amen."

Chapter 3

Cam

I'm standing outside of apartment 704. I had to bribe the security dude downstairs, to let me in with $100 and a nipple peek so she'd better open this freaking door.

I knock on the door. I knock again.

"Lyn, open this door. I'm not leaving and if I have to call and wake maintenance up, for a key, I will because—"

She snatches the door open. "What do you want?"

"Duh, you. Why else would I be searching for your chunky ass in the middle of the night, paying the little boy downstairs a hundred dollars and then letting him see my nipple. Girl, you better let me in."

"First off, I didn't ask you to come looking for me and how did you find where I live?"

She moves pass me. "Uh, you must have forgotten what I do for a living?" I stop. "Lyn, whose apartment is this because I know it isn't yours with no furniture."

"It's mine and I haven't gotten—never mind that. Why are you here?"

"To stop you from doing something stupid," I tell her

when I pick up some pills from the floor.

"Like you did?"

"Yep, exactly like I did, and I don't care about you being snippy with me, wanch because I am not about to let you go through what I did."

"Look Cam, I don't need advice from an addict who doesn't think she's an addict. I got me under control."

I laugh. "Sis, you're starting to sound like me but it's obvious you don't have shit under control. That's evident by this apartment. What is going on?"

"Do you remember when we were in LA and you told me to mind my business?"

"Yep."

"Well, now I'm telling you to mind yours."

"I can't do that because you know where that led me, and I will not stand by and watch you die. Not like this. Lyn, we've been through too much hell these last few months for this."

"Wow, so you're here on some captain save-a-hoe, shit?"

"Now, I'm supposed to be the hoe but if, for tonight, you want the role so be it because—"

"Cam, get out of my apartment."

"Nope." I kick off my shoes and sit, Indian style in

the middle of the floor. "Lyn, I'm not leaving you here. Not like this. Dang, now I see what Thomas has to go through, with me. I owe him an apology."

"Good, go and tell him now."

"Nope, I'm not leaving. I'm here to help you."

"I don't need your freaking help. Shouldn't you be with Shelby?"

"Shouldn't you be with Shelby?" I ask popping my lips.

"Cam, I am not in the mood to play with you."

"And I'm not in the mood to play with you either, boo-boo, so let's cut the bullshit." I pat the floor for her to sit. "What's going on?"

"Everything! Are you satisfied? Every-freak-ing-thing is going on!"

"When was the last time you slept?" I question.

"How can I sleep when all I see is Xavier's face. If not him, I see Kandis laughing or Paul's son. I can't sleep."

"Running isn't going to fix it. I know because I tried."

"What do you suggest then?"

"Restoration and recovery."

"What?"

"It might be recovery then restoration, I don't know but it's what Dr. Nelson, told me once in therapy. He said, sometimes you have to stage an intervention with self in order to survive. Or something like that. Lyn, you've been through the type of hell, I wouldn't wish on anybody, but you've got to recover and be restored."

"Why? What do I have to look forward to, Cam? My husband has a whole other family, including my daughter. What do I have?" she cries.

I stand up and walk over to her.

"You have you and you have us."

"I can't even look at myself in the mirror because this scar reminds me of that day."

"Then let's cover it up but you have to know, covering it won't erase the thoughts. Those, you have to come to grips with."

"Easier said than done."

"You don't think I know that? Hell, I can't even sleep on my back because it reminds me of those seven days, I spent in the hospital. Granted, I don't remember most of it but there are some things, I can't forget."

"Like?" she questions.

I sigh. "One day, I had a nightmare that Thomas had married Chelle—"

"Chelle?"

"She's the one we did the threesome with but anyway, they were married, and she was pregnant. TJ was gong-ho for it but Courtney, she was taking it the hardest. And," I pause, "she turned to drugs. She'd turned into me."

"Cam, I hear what you're saying but I don't know how to come to grips with this. Paul and I have been together since we were teenagers. My entire adult life was created around him and now, I don't know who I am."

"We can fix that, you know."

"How? We can either drink until you forget who you are, or we can figure out who Lynesha Darshan Townsend is. You know the one, before Paul."

She laughs.

"What's funny?"

"Don't you think it's crazy how you're so helpful and insightful to me and my problems, but you can't see your own?"

"Oh, I never said I didn't see them. I just ain't ready to give them up. Now, let's go because two of our best friends are going through something right now and they need us." I walk over and put my shoes back on.

"I can't."

"Girl, all this damn talking I just did and you're still not coming?"

"Cam, I'm tired and I am not in the right frame of mind to be what Shelby or Chloe needs, right now. But, will you stay, so I can sleep and then I'll go?"

"Of course, I will, but I hope you at least got an air mattress in this mother—"

"Camille," she laughs.

Ray

I open my eyes and see that I'm asleep on Anthony.

"Hey," he says kissing me on my forehead." I smile before sitting up to look at my watch.

6:12AM

"Man, I was hoping all of this was a nightmare." I wipe the tears from my face. "Anthony, how am I supposed to help her?"

"By being her strength."

"I'm trying but it's hard when I don't know what she's going through. Yesterday, she was a wife and now today, she's a widow. It's so unbelievable."

"Raylan, how did you feel when you found out your marriage was over?"

"I don't know," I shrug. "I was devastated, shocked, scared, hurt, angry and everything else."

"And how do you think Shelby feels?"

I take a second to think about his question.

"I guess the same, but it isn't the same. Justin cheated but he's still alive. Shelby has to bury her husband."

"I know and I'm not trying to minimize Shelby's pain. I'm only trying to get you to see that you can help her through this because of what you're going through. Raylan, when things end, whether it's a marriage, relationship or job; you experience a loss.

When you do, you go through the grieving process, the same as death. You go through questioning why, anger, depression and denial; until you finally get to a place of acceptance. Babe, you're grieving too. The good thing, you can both heal together. You're stronger than you know."

I touch his hand as his phone rings.

"Go on and take that. I'm going to check on Shelby."

I walk upstairs and don't see her in the bed, but I hear music coming from the closet.

"Your tears are just temporary relief. Your tears are just a release of the pain, sorrow, grief. Your tears are expressions that can't be controlled. A little crying now is alright, but after a while you won't have to cry no more; don't you worry, God's gonna wipe every tear away."

I turn the corner and see her asleep, with a shirt balled up in her hands. She's still whimpering.

"I won't have to cry no more, I won't have to cry no more, I won't have to cry no more when I reach the other shore. You promised me joy and peace, oh what a blessed, sweet relief."

I kneel beside her and touch her arm. She jumps.

"It's me."

She grips the shirt and cries. I sit in the floor and pull her head into my lap.

"Ray, I keep thinking this isn't real."

"I know, me too."

"I just don't understand how things happened so fast. One minute we're forgiving each other and the next he's gone. What am I supposed to do without my husband?"

I rock her because it's all I can do to keep from bursting into tears.

"We'll figure this out, one minute at a time."

"Do you think he suffered?"

"I don't know but I have to believe, he didn't."

"Man," she says as the same song plays over. She sits up and grabs her phone, turning the volume down. "Did you know Brian used to sing, in church, when he was younger?"

"No, why didn't you ever tell me that?"

"I don't know. I guess because he hadn't sung in a long time. He stopped, after his mom passed away. I never asked why but this song, Your Tears, by Paul Morton was his favorite. Now, I see why."

She closes her eyes and begins to sing, "your tears are just temporary relief. Your tears are just a release of the pain, sorrow, grief. Your tears are expressions that can't be controlled."

This time, I can't stop myself and I burst into tears.

"I'm sorry," I tell her.

She grabs my hand and sings, "a little crying now is alright, but after a while you won't have to cry no more; don't you worry, God's gonna wipe every tear away."

"Raylan," I hear Anthony calling.

"I'll be right back."

I walk out and meet him at the stairs.

"Mrs. Gray is here. She says the baby is fussing, restless and out of milk."

"I'll be right down." I go back to Shelby. She has her eyes closed and her hands lifted in the air. After a few seconds, she lowers them and wipes her face.

"Shelby, Mrs. Gray bought Brinae home because she's fussy and out of milk."

She stops the music and gets up.

"I need to take a quick shower and then I'll come down to get her."

I turn to walk out but she stops me.

"Ray, God is going to get us through this, right?"

"He most definitely will."

I get back downstairs and see Anthony holding the baby.

"Mrs. Gray," I say, walking over to give her a hug. "How are you?"

"Raylan, I don't know. This has been a shock. How is Shelby?"

"As well as we can expect. She's going to take a shower then come down. I'm going to fix coffee; would you like some?"

She nods before going into the living room. I stop and get my phone to see a missed call from Justin and a text from Cam, from over an hour ago.

CAM: I found Lyn. We'll be there as soon as she gets some sleep.

Shelby

I walk into the bathroom and when I see Brian's things, the way he left them, I cry out.

"Lord, you've got to help me. Please God."

I take a deep breath and turn the shower on.

Thirty minutes later, I've pulled my hair up, into a bun and gotten dressed, into some leggings and t-shirt. Walking downstairs, I stop when I see the living room has been cleaned.

"Shelby," Mrs. Gray stands, her eyes filling with tears.

"I know," is all I can say as I walk into her arms. "I know."

"What can I do?"

"You've done enough by taking care of Brinae. Thank you."

"I'll come back later to check on you all and if you need me to take her, I will," she tells me before leaving.

I go over to Anthony, to get the baby. "Thank you for staying but promise me, if Raylan allows, you'll be here for her. She's being strong for me and I need you to be strong for her." I tell Anthony before taking Brinae from his arms. She's whimpering as I put her on my shoulder, squeezing her.

"I will," he assures me.

I take the baby upstairs to the nursery and sit in the rocking chair, to nurse but she refuses. She starts to cry so I put her back on my shoulder and her little hand, wraps around my neck. I cover hers with mine.

"I know you can feel mommy's sadness. I miss daddy too, but he loved you, sweet pea and we're going to make it through this."

She stops crying.

She finally goes to sleep, and I lay her down. I touch the picture Brian had hung in her room before leaving out. I go into the kitchen.

"Are you hungry?" Ray asks.

"Not right now but I'll take some coffee."

"How's the baby?"

"She's finally asleep. As weird as it sounds, I think she knows Brian is gone. She wouldn't even nurse."

"Poor thing."

"Man, I need to call Brock, Brian's business manager and I have to get all the insurance information."

Ray sits the coffee cup in front of me.

"Thanks Ray. Have you talked to Justin?"

"Yeah, he's bringing the kids by later," I tell her.

"What about the girls?"

"Mike picked Kerri up, a little while ago. She's coming back after getting the bakery squared away. Cam went to check on Lyn and they'll be here later, too."

"Chloe? Has anyone talked to her?"

"I don't think so. Let me call Todd."

"Hey," Anthony says coming in. "I'm going to go home to shower and change clothes then I'll be back with food, for everybody."

She walks over and gives him a hug. "Thank you for being here." He kisses her on the forehead.

"If there's anything y'all need, before I get back, call me."

We both watch him walk out.

"He's a great guy, Ray."

"I know but he isn't mine," she sighs before grabbing her phone. Dialing Todd's number, she puts it on speaker.

"Hello," he says groggily.

"Todd, I'm sorry if I woke you."

"No, I was up. How are you Ray?"

"I've been better. How's Chloe and the baby?"

"They are both good. Chloe has some pain, throughout the night but she rested good after they got the medicine right."

"Is that Ray?" I hear Chloe asking in the background. "Let me talk to her."

"Wait," I tell him. "Have you told her about Brian?"

"Not yet," he sighs. "I was getting ready too."

"What are y'all whispering about? Give me the phone," she says. "Ray."

"Hey boo, how are you?"

"Tired and sore but otherwise good. Did y'all see the baby? Ray, she's gorgeous."

"No, we didn't get a chance too, but we will. Chloe, there's something I have to tell you and—"

"Just say it."

My leg is shaking.

"Chloe, Brian passed away, last night."

"What? Stop lying, Ray. Please tell me you're lying. Oh no," she begins to cry. "No Ray, this can't be true. What happened."

"He had a seizure."

"Where's Shelby?"

"I, um, I'm right here Chloe."

"Oh sister," she begins to sob.

"Chloe, I know it's hard, but I need you to calm down." I tell her. "Chloe, I'm okay and I need you to be. You have a little one who needs you."

She's still crying. "Ray, I'm going to let you go and calm her down." Todd says, taking the phone.

"I'm sorry," Ray says, crying. "I'm sorry."

I get up and walk over to her. "Raylan, you don't have to apologize, for being emotional. Brian was a part of all our lives so it's okay to mourn, even around me. Yes, the days to come will be hard, but Brian knew God, so I have no doubt that God received him in, last night. Yes, it hurts, but we will get through this. We have too."

"I'm in awe of you," she sniffs.

"It's God, all God."

Lyn

I roll over to Cam staring at me.

"How'd you sleep?"

"Damn, can you give me some space?"

"Girl, how much freaking space can you get, on this queen size air mattress?" she asks getting up. "Shoot, I got to peel myself off of it, just to pee."

"You didn't have to stay."

"Are we back on that again? Suh get up and take a shower, so we can go. And if you're going to stay here, you're getting some furniture."

"Whatever Camille."

"Whatever hell."

I get up and go into the bathroom and slam the door.

"Don't slam no door in this apartment, little girl." She says, and I can't do nothing but laugh. I turn on the water and go over to brush my teeth. Looking in the mirror, I see the scar on my neck.

"Jesus, you keep saving me but for what? You've got to show me the purpose in all this pain but for now, I'm going to trust you."

Two hours later, after stopping by Cam's for her to shower and get dressed; we're walking into Shelby's house.

"Hey," we say to Ray while Shelby walks, in circles on the phone.

"Who is she talking to?" I ask Ray who is holding Brinae.

"Brian's business partner. How are you?" she inquires, giving me a hug.

"I've been with this one, the last six hours, how do you think?"

"Oh hush," Cam says. "You know you like having me around."

"I do, just not all up in my space."

"Let's not even talk about your space, right now."

"Now, now, children," Ray laughs. "Are y'all hungry? Anthony bought some sandwiches and soup from Jason's Deli."

"Yes, please," Cam says.

"Whew," Shelby says coming over. "Hey y'all."

"Everything okay?"

"I had to break the news to Phillip, Brian's business partner and he didn't take it well. I asked him to tell the staff and handle things, for a few weeks. Man, I'm wondering if I should make an announcement on social media?"

"You can do that later because right now, you need some rest and once you tell the world, your phone and doorbell will never stop ringing."

The doorbell rings.

"See," Ray says.

"I'll get it." I open the door to Paul, Kelsey and Paul, Jr. asleep on his shoulder. "What are y'all doing here?"

"Lyn, I, uh, I didn't know you were going to be here." Paul stammers, "We only came to check on Shelby," he tells me.

"And you had to bring him."

"Lyn, he's my son and I couldn't leave him in the car but if it's too much, I'll come back."

"No, this isn't my house. You can do what you want. Besides, you're here now." I say, turning to walk off.

"Mom," Kelsey calls behind me. "Mom."

"What, Kelsey?" When I look at her, I notice her eyes are red and puffy.

"I'm sorry about Uncle Brian. I know these past few months have been hard and I'm sorry. I just wish things could go back the way they were," she tells me as tears drop from her eyes.

"Well they can't. Thank you for saying it though. Shelby is in the kitchen."

I turn to walk away but she rushes up behind me, wrapping her arms around me. "Mom, please," she screams loud enough for the girls to walk in. "I miss you," she sobs.

I close my eyes, trying to stop the tears before grabbing her hands to unlock them, from around my waist.

"I need you," she cries.

I stop and turn to her, backing away as she covers her face. Then, I hug her back and she cries harder. I squeeze her as my own tears flow. We stand there until I feel more arms around us.

"Dear God, we need you, more than ever. God, the pressure from this pain is getting heavy and we need you to give relief. God, your words says we can ask, in faith and you'll do it. Well, there's something that we need, at this very moment. We need healing from hurt, we need strength for this season of suffering, we need authority over this agony and we need comfort in place of this chaos and confusion.

God, we've faced a lot of hell, these past few months and the only way we can survive, is with you.

After rape, divorce, devastation, sickness and now death; we need you. God, you've kept us through all that and I know you're going to keep us now. Whatever the reason, for our suffering, we'll still trust you but, in the meantime, sustain. God, do it for us, please." Ray cries. "Please God, do it."

"God," Shelby says, "I don't understand but I won't question your will. All I want, need and desire is your comfort and strength; for all of us. Amen."

"Amen," we all say.

"We'll leave you all to talk."

"No," I state. "They're here to see Shelby. We're not here for me, not today."

"Lyn, I appreciate that but at this moment, we all need to recover and if this helps you, take it. I'm not going anywhere and I'm here, for them to love on, when y'all are done." Shelby tells me.

"And I'll lay him down," Ray says.

I watch them walk in different directions and then we go into the living room.

"Lyn, I miss you," Paul declares taking a step towards me and I step back. "I know this isn't the time to hash out, our differences and that wasn't my reason for coming here. However, I am glad to see you, after this morning."

"Look, I'm sorry about showing up like that. I was in a bad headspace and had it not been for Cam, I probably would have been somewhere across the ocean, instead of being here."

"Will you please come home?"

"Home? Paul, we don't have a home, not anymore."

"We can start over and buy another house."

"It isn't that simple, and you know it. You have a baby with a woman you've been with for over three years. She works at the company, I helped you start, from nothing. She has a relationship with my only daughter. She knows things about our life, no mistress should ever know. No Paul, we can't start over because we are over.

However, in order for me to move on, I've got to deal with this and that means, I need to forgive y'all. I'm not there yet but I'm going to work towards it. I love y'all," I say, looking from him to Kelsey, "I love y'all enough that if you needed my heart, I'd gladly give it, but I'm hurt and confused and need some time."

"Lyn," Paul walks closer and this time, I don't step back. "I'll give you all the time you need, and I'll always be here for you." He places my hand on his heart. "I've messed up, royally but you're the only woman who has my heart."

With that, he hugs me. I step back and wipe the tears. Kelsey then stands and hugs me.

"I love you," she declares.

"I love you too."

"Will you please take me off block, so I can call and text you?"

"Sure," I smile.

We walk into the kitchen, where Paul finally hugs Shelby.

"You have my deepest condolences," he tells her, "and if there's anything I can do, I'm here."

"Thank you," she says.

Ray comes around the corner with Paul's son.

"And who is this?" Shelby asks.

"This is my son, Paul Jr." Paul answers, looking at me.

I turn and walk out. Getting to the bathroom, he rushes in behind me, closing the door.

"I know seeing him hurts you and I'm sorry."

"Stop apologizing Paul, please. I'm fine."

"No, you're not."

"No, I'm not but I will be and I'm not your problem anymore."

"You were never my problem; you were my wife and I messed it up, but I miss the hell out of you." He kisses me, and I don't stop him. "I miss you so much."

When his hands go up my shirt, I flash back to the night of the attack.

"No, I can't." I start to breathe heavily. "I can't because all I see is him. The one who attacked me."

"Breathe," he tells me as I grip his shirt. "Breathe Lyn, you're okay and I'm right here."

I put my head on his chest and cry.

"I'm sorry I wasn't there to help you, that night, but if you'd allow me, I'd be right here to help you recover, now."

"I don't know how," I stutter through tears. "It hurts."

"Allowing me to be this close to you, is a start."

Chloe

Todd and I are standing outside of the incubator, watching the little person we created. I close my eyes and silently thank God for her.

"Are you okay?" he asks.

"Yeah," I wipe the tears, "just grateful for God sparing this little one."

"This little girl is a fighter and she's feisty." a nurse tells us, walking up. "Hi, my name is Rita and I'm one of the nurses taking care of baby Lark."

"How is she?"

"She's really good. We got the milk you pumped, and she's been holding it down."

"What is this orange tube?"

"It's her feeding tube. It's inserted through her mouth and down into her stomach. We have it hanging, at an angle, to allow the milk to flow smoother to keep it from upsetting her tummy. We also have her on oxygen and IV nutrition."

"When will we be able to hold her?" Todd questions.

"Here's her doctor now," she tells us.

"Hi, my name is Dr. Conner and this little lady is a feisty one."

We both laugh. "We've heard. Hi, I'm Chloe and this is Todd."

"It's nice to meet the both of you. As you know, she was born at thirty weeks gestation, weighing two pounds and six ounces but as you can see, she is able to breathe, for the most part, on her own. That's a blessing, in itself. We have her on a breathing machine, while her lungs grow stronger; oxygen, some IV nutrition as well as monitoring her temperature.

I know you were concerned about breastfeeding but she's not yet ready to be nipple fed because her stomach and intestines are still maturing. In a few days, we'll start to give her a pacifier to develop her eating and sucking muscles. Once they're good, we're move her to the breast. She's at a great starting point but we will keep her here, a while."

"When can we hold her?"

"You can start, skin to skin care, in about a week. You can work out the schedule with Rita as it's normally during feeding times. I know it's scary to see her like this but she's doing better than we could have anticipated. Whatever you've been doing, don't stop.

Here's my card," he hands it to Todd, "call me if you have any questions or concerns."

When he walks away, Rita comes back. "Have you all decided on a name yet?"

I look at Todd.

"Not yet," he says. "We weren't expecting her this early."

"That's okay, you take all the time you need because names have meaning and should not be taken lightly."

"Thank you."

We stay a little longer and then I head back to my room, to let Todd's mom and sister visit.

"Have you thought of a name?" Todd inquires.

"What about Tamah?"

"Tamar?"

"No, it's pronounced Tay-mah, nor mar. It's a biblical name that means blotting or wiping out." I tell him while I'm getting back into bed. "Your mom told me, the first day I met her, that this baby would bring me the joy I lost, this year. She was right."

"Tamah French," he says.

"Tamah Denise French," I correct.

A smile widens across his face before he comes

over and pulls me into a kiss.

"Girl, if you didn't just have my baby, I'd get you pregnant."

I laugh before there's a tap on the door.

"Oh my God," I yell when I see Lauren and Brittany. "What are you girls doing here?"

"We came to see you." Lauren says with tears in her eyes.

"Aw, don't cry. Come here."

They both come over and I give them a hug. "Girls, this is Todd. Todd this is Lauren and Brittany, my stepdaughters. They were the best thing Chris gave me, out of our relationship."

They both laugh.

"How did you know I was here."

"We overheard dad telling mom, so we begged him to bring us." I scrunch my nose. "I know, I know but it was better than an Uber."

"Where is the baby?"

"She's in the NICU. You can visit her, once Todd's mom and sister are done. The nurse, there, will tell you what you have to do, to go in because you'll have to wash your hands for a minute and put on gloves and a gown."

"I'm so excited."

"Are you excited that your mom is having another baby?"

"Uh, no! That's the last thing she needs." Lauren bellows.

"Lauren," I laugh, and she shrugs.

Todd's phone vibrates. "Babe, I'm going to walk mom and Taya out and I can show the girls where to go."

A short time later, Chris walks in.

"Hey," he says.

"Chris, please don't come with the dramatics today."

"I'm not. The girls wanted to see you, so I brought them."

"Why? Is it to bribe me out of money?"

"No and I apologize for that. I was stupid. Anyway, you don't look like a woman who just had a baby."

"Yea, well, I feel like it."

"You know this should have been us."

"What?" I ask.

"This should have been us," he repeats.

"We had our chance, but you didn't want it, remember?"

"I know, and I think about that mistake every day. I sure hope this new guy makes you happy."

"Todd and I are taking things slow, to get to know each other. I don't want to make the same mistake I made with you but yes, I truly believe this is my time for happiness."

"Good for you."

"Oh, I don't know if you've heard but Brian passed away yesterday."

"Brian? Shelby's husband?"

"Yes."

"No, I hadn't heard. What happened?"

"He has a seizure."

"Damn," he says. "That's messed up."

"I know but it makes me value life so much more. Chris, I know the relationship we had, wasn't meant although we tried to force it. Neither of us, really loved each other and I know, I only got married because I was tired of being alone. I'm sorry," I tell him. "I'm sorry for the part I played in this and I forgive you. I realize, the only way I can truly give Todd a chance, I have to move pass the past."

"You're right and I'm sorry too. When I met you, I'd been divorced for only a year, from Leslie and I knew I had no business being married again but with you I had stability. You were a strong woman and you knew what you wanted. Hell, you even tried to build me up, but I was too busy, being foolish and anything but a husband. Truth is, you scared me."

"I scared you? How?"

"You are never comfortable where you were. If there was something greater, you went for it. You set a goal and once it was reached, you moved to the next one, trying to figure out a way to beat it, better and faster.

Chloe, you're that kind of strong that don't really need a man and I thought, it was only a matter of time before you wised up and kick my ass out. I knew you were out of my league, but I didn't want to let you go because you made my life easy."

"Wow," I say. "Thank you for being honest but Chris, no matter how strong I am or appear to be, I still want to be loved. I want a man who makes sure my gas tank is full and my tires have the right amount of air. I want a man who will tell me to sit my ass down, won't be bothered by my attitude and he'll still ask me what I want to eat, when I'm mad.

I want a man who will love me on the days I'm not

strong or the times I don't meet a goal. I need a man who will cover me in prayer. I desire a man who isn't intimidated by my strength but he's proud of it because he knows, everything I do is not just me but for us."

"Is pretty boy capable of doing that?" he smirks.

"You're damn right," Todd says from behind Chris, "and I plan on showing her, if she'll have me. But I've got to thank you for messing up because had you not, I wouldn't have found her."

Chris looks at Todd for a second then he reaches out his hand.

"Treat her better than I did," he tells him.

"Oh, I plan too."

"Uh, hello, I'm right here."

"Hush woman," they both say.

Kerri

"Hey," Mike says, walking into the bedroom. "Ms. D has MJ—you okay?" he stops.

"That could be me," I reply, wiping tears.

"What do you mean?"

"I could be in Shelby's shoes, Mike. I could have been burying you. Why did God spare us and not her?"

"Babe, I can't answer why God does what He does but Bible tells us that life is, but a vapor and no man knows the day nor the hour. All we can do is be ready."

"How can you ever be ready for death?"

"Be ready, as in prepared when God calls your name. Babe, nobody is ever ready to say goodnight to a loved one because death is something we can never prepare for."

"I know but I'm hurting for her," I cry. "I have to watch my best friend grieve and a little girl, grow up who may not remember her daddy. Yet, I feel bad because while they're mourning, I'm thankful.

Thankful because when I think back over these past few months, my soul is crying out with thanks, for a God who kept us. While you were bar and bed hopping, God kept you. While you stood in an alley with a gun in your face, God kept you. While I was in my mess, God kept me."

He takes my hand.

"Kerri, if we had the answer to everything God did, we wouldn't need Him. Yet, while we may not understand, being thankful for God's grace, does not take away your ability to grieve with and be there for Shelby. If the roles were reversed, I'm sure she'd feel the same way. Now, you take a moment and get your tears out because your sister needs you."

"When did you become so wise?" I smile, rubbing his face.

"Being in that therapy center, for three months, allowed me to gain a deeper relationship and longing for God. The first two nights, I was there, I had to go through detox. Kerri, it was bad, physically and mentally. I couldn't sleep because of nightmares. I was jumpy and would fluctuate between depression and anxiety. I had nausea and vomiting, sweating and headaches but I knew it was what I had to do, to get back to you. I'm stronger because of what I went through, not because of why.

And I believe God was preparing us, all of us, for

this because He knew we'd never make it through, then but we're stronger now. Think about it, everybody's house was affected but now, we're all on the road to recovery and restoration. Some of us, are farther along but that's to help those, like Shelby, who's recovery is just beginning. We have to trust God, especially when we don't understand."

I wrap my arms around him. "I love you."

"I love you too."

★★★★★

I walk into the bakery's kitchen. The young lady, who I hired, to work up front has been a blessing.

"Hey, Mrs. Kerri, how are you?"

"I'm good Selena, how have things been, this morning?"

"Great. I left a list of things we're either out of or close to being out of."

"Thanks."

"Is there anything you need me to do?" she questions.

"No," I tell her. "I'm going to get started on baking but if you need me, holler."

I take the list, begin to set up my mixing bowls,

turning on the ovens and getting all the things I need to bake.

A few hours later, I hear someone clear their throat. I look up to see Adrian.

"Hey," I say wiping my hands on the towel tucked into my apron before going over to give him a hug.

"Hey, it's smelling good in here."

"Well, you know how I do. How are you? It's been a while since I've laid eyes on you. Everything okay?"

He sighs. "Yea, just dealing with some personal issues. What about you? I heard about your friend's husband."

"The same."

"Anything I can do?"

"Pray, that's all I've been doing since it happened. Life changes so fast, you know."

"Unfortunately, I do," he replies. "I came by because I wanted you to know, I'm closing the coffee shop."

"Why?" I ask, surprised.

"I'm going through a divorce and my wife will not allow me to buy her out."

"Oh no, that's awful."

"I'm going to reopen once everything is settled.

She's become someone I don't recognize."

"That can happen, I know because I was where you are, months ago. Thank God, Mike got help."

"Sharon is bipolar, and she stopped taking her meds. She doesn't want to admit that she needs help. I've tried all I can, to help her, but she's fighting me on every hand and I'm tired."

"Then you have to do what's best for your sanity, Adrian. I know you must be hurt, over the coffee shop but you'll get the chance to reopen. Don't look at this like losing but take it as an opportunity to remodel and recover."

He smiles. "I never thought of it like that. Thank you."

"No problem."

"I'm going to get out of here and let you get back to work. I only wanted to check on you and tell you, in person, in case I don't see you before the Coffee Spot officially closes on December 31st. I also didn't want you making all of those extra pastries."

"Wait, you're the one that has been buying me out on Monday's?"

"Yes. I asked the young lady not to tell you. I knew we'd decided not to work together but your pastries are too delicious."

"Wow, okay."

"Take care Kerri."

"Wait," I tell him. "Can I pray for you? You took the time to pray for me, when I was going through. Will you, at least, let me do that for you?"

I walk over and grab his hands.

"God, your word says to encourage one another and at this moment, I come asking for strength to encourage my friend. He's your child, one whom you've called to walk among men but sometimes, they need prayer too. Therefore, I'm asking you God, to give him strength to survive.

Walk with him and keep his mind. Cover and protect him, surrounding him with those who can uplift and not bring him down. Surround him with those who can pray for him, when he can't find the words. Do for him, God, what he cannot do for himself. Thank you Father and we know that everything will work out for the good of those who love you. We love you and we trust you, God. Amen."

"Amen," he smiles. "Thank you, Kerri. I really appreciate that."

"You're welcome and here, take a few cupcakes

with you. They won't fix your problems but they're good."

Chapter 4

Brian's funeral

Celebration of Life

Brian Avery James

April 8, 1981 – December 19, 2018

High Point Christian Center

785 Alabama St.

Memphis, TN 38104

January 5, 2019 1:00 PM

Pastor Magnolia Reeves, Officiating

Shelby

I stand at the door of the church, staring ahead at the dark matte blue casket that holds my husband's body. Blue is, was his favorite color because he loved the Tennessee Titans.

As the music to, 'I Shall Wear a Crown,' plays, Ray nudges my arm, to let me know its time to walk down the aisle. When I get to him, I rub my hand over his jaw.

"Man, how I miss you," I tell him, gripping the sides of the casket. "We were going to grow old together. You weren't supposed to leave me."

I feel Ray's hand on my back.

"Lord," I cry out before laying my head on her shoulder. "Sister, this hurts every muscle in my body."

"I know baby but we're right here. You can let it out and we'll be right here to catch you."

I put my hand on his chest, one last time.

After the soloist sings, "When I see Jesus," Pastor Reeves walks to the podium.

"I had the privilege of meeting Brian and his family, about three months ago. To some, this may not be interesting but three biblically means divine wholeness, completion and perfection. What does that mean? It means God had this thing worked out, perfectly, His way.

Sure, I know we want to question God on why He'd allow this to happen. How could he allow a thirty-seven-year-old man to die, suddenly? I mean, doesn't God know the plans you've made? Doesn't God know, this hurt? Doesn't God know the pain this has caused?" she pauses.

"My brothers and sisters, God knows, for it was God who made the decree, in the Garden of Eden, to Adam. He said in *Genesis 3:19*, *"By the sweat of your brow you will eat your bread, until you return to the ground—because out of it were you taken. For dust you are, and to dust you shall return."*

I know it doesn't stop your pain and while I could stand here trying to make you feel better about losing a loved one, the reality is, death happens and there is nothing I can potentially say that can take away what you are going through.

I wish I could pray the perfect prayer to stop your pain. I wish, my being here for you was all that is needed to erase the confusion in your mind, but it isn't.

This is why I will not sugar coat the message this morning, death hurts but it's not what it seems.

We look at the obituary with the face of our loved one and we think we will not see him again but it's not what it seems. We look at the casket, holding the physical body of Brian and we see finality but it's not what it seems. We look at the emptiness of the home he'll never walk in again and we want to break but it's not what it seems.

For it is in the bible that is says in *Ecclesiastes 12:7, "before the dust returns to the ground from which it came, and the spirit returns to God who gave it."*

This is why I have to tell you this afternoon, it's not what it seems. See, you think death is final when death is just rest. You think death is the end when death is the path that some of us have to take to get to glory, where our life truly begins.

Does it make it easy? No but it happens. And while we want to question God, He doesn't owe us an explanation on why He does what He does, when He has the ability to repossess what belongs to Him, whenever He feels like it."

*****

The funeral is a blur to me as I sit and stare at the coffin, knowing it's final. I wish I could get Brinae, get in bed and sleep; only waking up to know this was a terrible, horrible nightmare.

"Shelby, I am so sorry for your loss."

"Shelby, your husband was a good man."

"Shelby, Brian will definitely be missed."

"Shelby, if there is anything we can do, please call us."

I am so tired of hugging people and hearing them say the same thing over and over. *I'm sorry for your loss.*

"Why are you sorry?"

"Shelby, who are you talking to?" Ray ask, coming up to me.

I hadn't realized that I was talking out loud. "I just don't understand why people say they are sorry for your loss? Does that make sense?"

"It's a common thing to say. They're sorry for everything you have to deal with, that's all."

"I know but don't feel sorry for me because I don't need pity. What I need is prayer for strength and comfort."

"They're praying, sweetie."

She leads me to the family car. We ride to the cemetery in silence. Brian's brother didn't show up, but I hadn't expected him to. They'd barely spoken to each other ever since their mom passed away four years ago, but I had my girls and they were enough.

Mrs. Gray and her daughter have been a godsend, for taking care of Brinae. Chloe was released from the hospital, after a few days although the baby will be there a little while longer. I tried to talk her out of coming today, but she was adamant about being here.

The car slows down as we pull into the cemetery.

Brian's final resting place.

My heart starts to beat faster, and my leg begins to shake, knowing today I bury my husband and the father of my baby girl. I look down at the obituary, at the picture I chose of him.

It was one we took, a few months back, while playing around at home. It turned out so good that I had it printed. Never on a million stars would I have thought it would be used for this.

"Oh God," I say as tears flood my face. "This is so hard." I clinch the obituary to my chest.

The driver of the car opens the door, for us to get out but Cam requests a few minutes.

"This makes everything so final. If I could just see him again, talk to him and feel his arms around me," I cry. "I should have taken him up on that dance. What am I supposed to do?"

Ray remove my shades and wipes the tears from my face with a tissue. "If I could take your pain, I would, don't you know that?"

"I know, but I wouldn't wish this type of pain on my worst enemy. It hurts so bad, Ray. It hurts to breathe."

"What can we do? Just tell us and we'll do it," Cam asks, crying.

"I wish I knew." I lay my head back on the seat. "I wish I knew."

I take a deep breath.

After a few minutes, we finally make it out of the car and to the burial site. I look around at the number of people who'd come, and it makes me smile to know Brian's life touched so many people.

I listen as Pastor Reeves begins to speak.

"Even when we've had to look in the face of death, we thank You, God, for Your gift of eternal life. For we know that although we are separated now, we thank You for the eternal reunion we so eagerly wait to have in Heaven. We thank You for Brian's life here on this earth, and we recognize that the body that lies before us is not him but rather the earthly house in which he lived.

So, we acknowledge that he is resting, even now, from the pain of sickness and the cruelness of this mean world. We anticipate the day when spirit and body shall be united again at the coming of the Lord, and we find great comfort in knowing that we shall forever be together with you, in Heaven.

We thank You Father, that in the days, weeks, and months to come, these realities and the abiding presence of Your Spirit will especially strengthen, sustain, and comfort the family and friends. Let us pray."

I close my eyes but all I see is Brian's face from the morning I woke to him watching me sleep. He's smiling, and I reach to touch his face, but Cam taps me on the leg. It's time to place our flowers on his casket.

I take a deep sigh and stand, readjusting my skirt and trying to steady my legs. The only family Brian had, biological, was his brother and since he didn't show, each one of the girls and some of Brian's coworkers hold a red rose.

We all stand at the casket.

Pastor Reeves begins to speak again, "To you, O Lord, we commend the soul of your dearly beloved servant, Brian. Forgive whatever sins he may have committed, on earth and welcome him into your everlasting peace.

For we count it all joy to know that it has pleased you, our Heavenly Father, to take unto Himself our beloved husband, father, brother and friend. We therefore commit his body to the ground, earth to earth, ashes to ashes, dust to dust, looking for the blessed hope and the glorious appearing of the great God in our Savior Jesus Christ."

We take our seats.

"This now concludes the burial of our dear brother Brian James. May the God of peace, who through the blood of the eternal covenant brought back from the dead our Lord Jesus, that great Shepherd of the sheep, equip you with everything good for doing his will, and may he work in us what is pleasing to him, through Jesus Christ, to whom be glory for ever and ever. Amen.

We thank you for taking the time to share your condolences today and we ask your continued prayers for the family in the days, weeks, months, and years to come. You may now return to your cars."

Chapter 5

A month later

Chloe

"Hey," I say walking into Todd's apartment. "What's this?"

"Our first date," he says pointing to the table he had set, in the eat-in kitchen.

"I thought we were meeting to talk about the results of the DNA test and plans."

"I told you I didn't need that test because I already knew she was mine. My mother has been saying it since that day at the photoshoot. Although I acted like a jerk," he shakes his head. "And what plans?"

"Co-parenting."

"Chloe, we're raising our daughter, together. Besides, my mother would kill me, otherwise. Do you know how excited she is about her first grandchild?"

"Uh, you should see the nursery," I chuckle. "She's purchased so much stuff, I don't think I'm going to have any room for her crib. Which reminds me, will you have time to put it up or should I pay the people at the store?"

"Ms. Lark, we can do nursery things tomorrow and you better not pay a dime for a stranger to put my daughter's crib together. Now, tonight is about us. I know, with both of us spending time at the hospital, you trying to work from home and me, in meetings; we'll never get to this so, wah-lah."

"Did you say wah-lah?" I laugh.

"Yea, I couldn't think of anything else," he joins me in laughing. "Now, come, sit and eat." he orders. "I have water, tea and lemonade. I wasn't sure if you were drinking wine yet."

"Lemonade is fine."

He brings over the food before going back to get our drinks.

"This smell and looks amazing."

"It's pecan crusted tenderloin with wild rice and green beans. You aren't allergic to nuts, are you?"

"No."

"Whew. See, this is why I wanted us to get to know one another. I was hoping it would be before, Little Miss. Tamah arrived but we still have time before she comes home."

I smile before we bow, and he says grace.

I cut into the tenderloin and put a piece in my mouth. "This is good, better than the hospital food, we've been eating."

"Thanks."

"Okay, since we're getting to know each other, I'll go first. My name is Chloe Alexa Grant Lark. I'm 37 and I own and operate Truth Magazine. I've been married once and divorced. Tamah, is my first biological child along with my two stepdaughters, Lauren and Brittney.

Before all the chaos begin, in our lives, I hadn't been to church in a while but I'm leaning towards joining High Point because I love Pastor Reeves' ministry. What else? Oh, I take relationships, very serious and I'm normally not a cheater. Scouts honor," I tell him holding up my fingers.

"May I ask, why you cheated on your husband?"

"He stopped caring. I met Chris, when he came to my office to service my printer, one day. We hit it off and started dating. We did so, for two years before getting married. I knew he wasn't the right person for me, but all of my girls were married, and I was tired of being alone."

"Did you love him?"

"I think I did but I don't know because, to be honest, he was my first real relationship," I state with air quotes. "I was raised, mostly in foster homes and I'd never seen a real relationship between a man and wife. I was treated fine, in the homes I lived in, but I never truly knew love.

Then I met Chris and he acted as if, he loved me, but I realized, it wasn't love, for me; he loved my stability. I guess, I can say that I loved his companionship until he stopped giving it to me. Anyway, we're divorced. It was final day I came to your hotel. Enough about me, who is Todd French?"

He wipes his mouth and lays the napkin in his lap, while I pick up my fork. "My full name is Todd Darnell French. I'm the youngest of two and until recently, I lived in Gatlinburg. My mom, sister and I went there, one year on vacation and I knew that's where I wanted to be. I'd lived there for seven years and operated Crawford's, a restaurant named after my mother's maiden name, for over five years. I've never been married but I was in a relationship, for two years."

"Was she the one who—"

"Lied about being pregnant? Yeah. Thing is, she was pregnant, just not by me. But she kept up that lie until she pushed him out knowing she wouldn't be able to explain why my son had blonde hair and blue eyes. He turned out to be her boss' baby.

It was heartbreaking but that was three years ago. Now, I'm looking for the woman who I can grow old with. One who, hopefully, likes all of the Marvel and Fast & Furious movies. One who wants more than one baby, preferably three, enjoys taking spontaneous trips and laughing."

"Well, I haven't seen the Marvel movies," I tell him before covering my face with the napkin.

"That's it, this date is over. Get your things. Woman, are you kidding me? You've never seen Avengers, Thor, Spiderman, nothing."

"Oh, I've seen Spiderman, the old one. Does that count?"

"Jesus, you're killing me. Are you open to seeing them?" he asked with a look of confusion and I stare at him. "Well?"

"Of course, only if you agree to watch some scary movies with me."

"Deal," he replies reaching his hand across the table for us to shake. "What about food? Are you picky or allergic to anything?"

"No known allergies and heck no, I'll try anything once."

"I like that. What about love? You said you didn't know about real relationships but what are you looking for, as far as love?" he inquires.

"I want real love. The kind that gives me butterflies, every time I see my husband because his eyes shows me that I'm all his, every time he looks at me. I want the love that withstands an argument, the kind that can agree to disagree and is not afraid to speak its mind.

Todd, I want the kind of love that I can't wait to get home to. Love that will look for ways to refresh itself instead of growing tired and giving up. I want the kind of love that makes me want to fight for because it's just that damn good. Oh, and bomb sex even when we're in our sixties."

"Damn," he says. "I, I was trying to think of a rebuttal but I'm just going to say, ditto."

We laugh.

"Seriously Chloe, I want all the same things. My mom and dad were married 32 years before he passed away and I saw that man, cherishing her until he could no longer keep his eyes open. That's the kind of love that's within me. And I know that we're still learning about each other, but I hope you'll give me a chance to love you."

"How do you know I'm the one for you?" I ask.

"I'd been celibate for three years, before meeting

you but that night, at the cabin, there was a force so strong, I couldn't resist it. Chloe, I know God doesn't agree with adultery, but I'd resisted every woman who has come on to me, over those years but I couldn't resist you.

And, you'd better know that I did some serious praying afterwards," he laughs, "because I knew you were meant for me. I didn't know how things would work because I couldn't ask God to break up your marriage but man, I thought about it. Instead, I asked God to forgive me and then I asked Him to show me if you were mine."

"And?"

"You showed up at the photoshoot, throwing up over everything and telling me you were pregnant with my child."

"The crazy thing, that was the first time the smell of food had ever made me sick."

"I knew it," he exclaims jumping up.

"Then why were you a jackass?"

"Woman, I was scared. God was giving me exactly what I'd asked Him for and it was blowing my mind. I'm sorry about that, by the way."

"Mmhmm… where do we go from here?"

"We go anywhere you want, until you're ready to be my wife."

Cam

"Good morning," Thomas says, walking up behind me at the kitchen counter.

"Good morning, Mr. Shannon."

"I love you," he tells me.

I turn around to look at him.

"What?"

"I love you too," I stammer, "but it's been a while since I've heard you tell me that."

"I know and with everything that happened with Brian," he pauses, "that could have been me."

"Thomas—"

"No, let me finish. I realized just how close I was to losing you, yet God allowed you to recover and now, I think it's time for us to be restored."

"Really?"

"Yea. You've been going to therapy and over the last couple of months, you've changed. I just want us to be happy again."

"I want that too."

He kisses me, and I begin to pull his shirt out of his pants. "Make love to me."

He kisses me again but steps back. "I will tonight but I have to go. I got court at nine."

"Thomas—"

"I promise, I'll give you all of big daddy, tonight when you move back into our bedroom."

He kisses me again, grabs his briefcase and walks out.

*****

"Wow, that was amazing." Joshua, the law student who has been shadowing me the last week, exclaims when the courtroom is empty.

It's been two weeks since Brian's funeral and me being back at work. God, I've missed the adrenaline of being in a courtroom.

I smile at him.

"I mean, the way you caught that man up, in his lies. You did it in a nice, nasty kind of way. Dang, you made me want to confess and I wasn't even there."

"What can I say, I love what I do."

"It shows, you were amazing."

We're packing up when Lewis, Judge Alton's bailiff comes over. "Mrs. Shannon, Judge Alton would like to see you before you leave."

"Thanks Lewis." I turn back to Joshua.

"Joshua, thank you for being here this week. I hoped you've learned more about the law and you'll keep us in mind, once you graduate.

"Oh, most definitely. Your law firm is my top pick."

"Great. Then I look forward to working with you."

He gets his things and bounces out the courtroom. I finish packing up my computer and files before grabbing all my things and walking to Judge Alton's office.

"Hey," he says when I walk in. "Welcome back. I was glad to see you on my docket again."

"Why, did you miss me?" I ask smiling.

"Of course, you know I can never get enough of your smart-ass mouth," he says closing the door. "But seriously, how are you? I have seen you since that night at the cigar bar and you're looking very good, by the way."

"Thank you and I am doing very well. Glad to be back at work."

"Hmm, how can you still smell this sweet after being in court all day?" He kisses my neck.

"Is this why you needed to see me?" I ask laughing.

"Yea," he replies in between kisses before

grabbing my hand and placing it between his legs.

I close my eyes, squeezing him. "I can't do this," I tell him, barely above a whisper. "I'm trying to repair my marriage and I can't do that bent over your desk."

He steps back. "I'm sorry. I never want to be the reason your marriage doesn't work."

"I know, and you don't have to apologize. I should have told you when I walked in." I can't even make eye contact, with him, for looking at the bulge in his pants. "Damn it." I move from the desk and begin pacing. "I need to get out of here."

"Wait, I'm sorry."

"No, you didn't know but thank you for respecting me enough to not push."

"Always," he says fixing his pants. "Where are you headed? Care to join me for a cigar and drink?"

"No thanks. I'm going to stop by and check on my friend Shelby then head home."

"She's the one whose husband passed? How is she doing?"

"She's getting better, taking it a day at a time. Losing a spouse is a hard pill because it changes the total dynamic of your life."

"I know," he sighs. "It's been three years for me and

sometimes it feels like yesterday. Please let her know she's in my prayers."

"I will." I grab my purse. "Thanks for the meeting. I will see you later."

I open the door and walk out, only to run into Thomas.

"Camille, where are you coming from?"

"I just finished up a case and needed to talk to Judge Alton about something."

He looks back at the door. "Is that all you were doing?"

"Yea, wait, are you serious?"

He moves closer to me. "Is this because I wouldn't have sex with you, this morning."

"Wow, are we seriously doing this? I thought we'd moved pass this?"

"Have we, Camille?" he questions looking me up and down.

"Nothing happened, we were only talking. You can go and ask yourself. Better yet, you want to smell my pus—"

"That's enough," he says grabbing my hand and looking around when I go to raise my skirt.

"No, this is enough. You were talking all that shit

about restoration, this morning and now, not even eight hours later, you're accusing me."

"Whatever Camille, I was only asking."

"No, you were accusing. Am I going to have to explain every time you see me with a man? If so, I can't do this."

"Can we talk about this when we get home?"

"No, I'm talked out. Don't wait up for me."

Ray

"Hey Ray, it's good to have you back in the office," Shelly says walking in.

"It feels good to be back. How was your holiday?"

"It was great. My parents and I went on a sixteen-day cruise to Hawaii."

"Sixteen days, on a boat? No thank you."

"It was good because we got to see like seven different ports of Hawaii. You should try it."

"I don't know," I laugh, "but what's on the schedule for today?"

"Mr. Johnson has a meeting with a Mr. Trapp and he's asking you to sit in."

I roll my eyes. "What time?"

"Two, in the conference room attached to his office."

"Thanks. Is that all?"

"Yep, other than the hundreds of emails you have to go through," she smiles.

"Don't remind me. Thanks Shelly."

After working, for a few hours, I grab my wallet to head downstairs for lunch. Opening the door, my phone buzzes, on the desk but deciding against it, I step out and come face to face with Justin's mom, Verdean.

"Verdean, what are you doing here?"

"Raylan, I'm sorry to show up here but I've been trying to call you. Can we talk?"

I look at my watch. "Sure, I have a few minutes."

I step back to allow her to walk in before I close the door.

"What's so urgent that you'd come here?" I ask.

"Justin is dating, a man," she says whispering the last part.

"That's what gay people do, Verdean."

"No, this isn't right. You've got to stop him."

"Stop him? This isn't a child running into the middle of the street, after a ball. You got me so messed up. Lady, you allowed me to marry Justin, knowing full well, he's gay."

"He's not, it's just a phase."

"A phase? A phase is when you're having a mid-life crisis and you buy a drop top Maserati, you can't afford or turn into a hoe, for a weekend. This though? This isn't a phase. Verdean, your son is gay and always has been. While, I can't be mad at you, for his actions, I am upset that you didn't tell me."

"There was nothing to tell. Raylan, if Justin was gay, why would y'all have been married all this time?"

"Because he's been trying to prove something to you."

"No," she shakes her head, "this is him acting out because you cheated."

"What?" I laugh. "Are you freaking serious? Did Justin tell you that?"

"Of course."

"Well, let me clarify a few things, dear mother-in-law. Number one, I didn't cheat until after he did. Number two, this isn't acting out, he's being who he is. And number three," I open up the picture app on my phone, scroll to the video and press play, "he's all the way gay."

Her mouth drops as she stares at the screen. I stop it. "This isn't an act and it's time for you to go."

"That video means nothing. Will you stop and listen to me? Why are you being a bitch?"

My head snaps around. "There's something seriously wrong with you and I'm going to let that slide because if I was being a bitch, I would've cussed your ass out by now, for not only ruining my life but that of my children.

Lady, you're certifiable crazy, if you think I'd ever take Justin back, knowing he likes to be penetrated through his back door. Furthermore, he ain't my problem, anymore. We're divorced. Now, get the hell out of my office."

"You're going to regret this."

"Regret what, exactly? Verdean, have you even talked to your grandchildren? Do you know how bad this has affected them? No, because you're too busy trying to cover up the truth. Your son is gay!"

"No, no, you're wrong. He's not gay"

"You're right," I cave. "He's not gay just like you aren't crazy. Goodbye Verdean."

I open up the door and wait for her to walk through it before I close it. I really, I mean like really, really; wanted to slam it but I'm at work. I close out the picture app and dial Justin's number, putting the phone on speaker, while I gather my things.

"Hey Raylan, I wasn't expecting your call," he answers.

"And I wasn't expecting your mother to show up at my job, so we're even. Where are you? We need to talk."

"Uh, can—"

"Hell no, this can't wait. Either you meet me, or I'll come to where you are."

"Fine," he relents. "Where?"

I look at my watch. "The house. We have about two hours before the kids get home."

I text Anthony to let him know I can't make the meeting because something important came up.

Twenty minutes later, I am pacing in the living room, when Justin walks in the front door.

"Ray, before you say it, I apologize for my mother."

"Fuck that, how dare you act like, the only reason you cheated, with a man, was because of me. Your lifestyle is not because of me and you need to stop lying! Your mother may have covered for you, all these years, but I won't."

"I know and I'm sorry. I tried to talk to her but—"

"But nothing. You're a grown man who needs to stand up to his mommy. Period!"

He sits on the couch, with his head in his hands.

"Justin, I'm tired," I sigh. "This past year has been draining, mentally and physically and I can't go on like this."

"I know and I'm sorry."

"Will you please say something else, besides that?"

"What would you like me to say?"

"Say you're gay, to YOUR MOTHER! For the love of all things holy, it's true. Justin, we can't move pass this if you're still going to lie about who you are. The kids are willing to extend you grace because they understand, shit happens. Even this. However, it does no good if you're going to continually lie, to save face with your mother. Aren't you tired?"

"More than you know."

When he answers that, I realize he's crying.

"Ray, I know I need to tell my mother the truth, but I couldn't bear to see the same hurt and disappointment, in her eyes that I saw in yours. I don't know if I could take it."

"Justin, you had the balls to tell me, you didn't love me; untuck them again and tell her the truth. Hell, your mother is eighty years old."

He looks at me. "You know she's not that old."

I shrug, "well, she looks like it. Either way, she's too old to keep up this foolishness. Yes, I know how it is to want the love and acceptance of your parents but you're almost forty and at some point, you've got to think about you."

"You're right and before you called, I'd already made up my mind to do that, even if it meant her cutting me off."

"Then why didn't you start with that, instead of allowing me to go on and on?"

"I've met someone, Ray," he blurts.

"Good for you but you need to be telling Verdean, not me."

"I plan on it but I'm telling you because I want you and the kids to meet him."

"No thanks. Justin, I'm all for giving you grace, forgiving you and eventually, remembering what you did to me, differently but I'm drawing the line. I will not condone your choice of being gay."

"You just said I needed to own my truth. Damn, which is it?" he stands up.

"Hold on, remove the bass from your voice, pooh. Yes, you should own your truth, but I will not sit here and act like I'm cool with you being gay. It's your life and your choice but it also goes against the God I serve."

"I'm not asking for your approval because my life

choices and repentance is between me and God. I only want you to meet him, should the children decide they want to be a part of our lives."

"I'll think about it."

He looks at his watch. "Is it okay if I stay until the kids get home?"

"Sure. I'm going to change clothes and fix dinner before I go to check on Shelby."

"Wait," he says causing me to turn back. "Did you tell your mom, when she was here?"

"No, I told her before. Why?"

"It was the way she acted towards me at Brian's funeral. She was stand-off-ish."

"She's mad at you for hurting her only daughter."

"Is it alright if I call her?"

"Justin, do whatever you have to do, to recover you but this is the last conversation I will have about it, you and your mother."

Lyn

Today is the first time I've been back at my store, since the attack and although it's been four months, my stomach still tensed up, pulling into the parking lot.

My hand is shaking as I put my key in the back door. I take a deep breath and grab the handle, but I couldn't open it.

Closing my eyes, trying to fight back the tears, I realize, in order to overcome my fears, I'd got to face them.

I take another deep breath.

"Lyn."

I open my eyes when I hear Jo's voice, behind me.

"You got this," she says, "one step at a time."

I jump when she touches my shoulder. A few seconds later, I pull the door open and it looks completely different, thanks to the repainted walls and new laminate flooring.

"Jo, this looks amazing," I tell her when we walk in. "Thank you for doing this for me. If I can't erase the nightmares, while I sleep, the least I can do is erase what I can physically see, when I'm woke.

"Amen," Jo says as we're walking into my office. "I know it's hard being here, but you took the first step and that's the hardest."

"Girl, who you telling?" I smile. "Jo, thank you for everything, these past few months. Without you, I wouldn't have been able to make it."

"Lyn, I should be thanking you for trusting me with your baby. When I met you, twelve years ago, I was fresh out of jail and didn't have a dime to my name. Our first meeting, I was trying to steal your credit card and you caught me," she laughs. "Instead of sending me back to jail, you helped me recover. In a way, you helped to restore me.

You," she pauses when she gets emotional, "you gave me another chance. If it hadn't been for you and God, I'd either be back in jail or dead. Yet, you trust me, and I'll never be able to thank you."

I wipe the tears, "Girl, when we met, I was just as broken as you. Paul and I were starting his company and I was selling clothes out of my garage, to help make ends meet. That day, we crossed paths, it was us saving each other. I helped you because listening to your story, helped me.

Six years later, when I was finally able to purchase

a building, you were the first person I had in mind, to help me. Jo, you thank me, each time you take care of my baby."

She comes over and we hug.

"Whew," we both say.

"Thank you for making me cry, this early in the morning. Now, let's get some work done."

She pulls her laptop up and we start going through inventory and accounting. Two hours later, we finish just in time to open the store.

I stay in my office while she goes up front. I pick up my phone to call Paul but decide against it. Since that day at Shelby's, we've been texting, every now and then. Kelsey and I even had lunch, a few weeks back.

Baby steps.

I haven't seen Paul, in person, but I'm trying to forgive him. He says things are over with Kandis and they are co-parenting.

I pick up my phone, but I hear the back door open.

"Jo," I call out, "is that you?"

When there's no answer, I stand and grab a mannequin's arm from the table and walk to the door. I see a shadow and when it gets close, I swing.

"Whoa, Lyn, it's me," Paul screams.

"You scared me. Why didn't you answer when I called out?"

"I didn't hear you because I had my earpiece in."

"What are you doing here?"

He takes the arm away from me. "I came to see if I could take you to lunch, not get beat to sleep."

"Then you should have said something," I shrug, looking at my watch. "I don't have time, for lunch but I would like your help with something."

"Anything?"

"I'm having some furniture delivered to my apartment, between two and four. Will you meet me there? I'm just not comfortable doing it by myself."

"Of course, what's the address and I'll meet you there."

I walk back into my office and write the address down. I hand it to him. "Thank you, Paul."

"No thanks needed. I'll see you at two."

*****

At ten minutes to two, Jarvis, from security called for authorization to let Paul up. I wait until he knocks before I open the door.

"Hey," I say to him.

"Lyn, this is a very nice complex but why are you just having furniture delivered?" he looks at me with concern. "What have you been sleeping on?"

"An air mattress but that's because I wasn't sure if I was going to stay here."

"Here, as in this apartment or city?"

"City."

"Lyn—"

"No Paul, I don't want to rehash everything. I'm getting better now and leaving wouldn't have changed the things I needed to deal with, anyway. Covering up my problems, won't make them disappear. Anyway, today is a new day." I smile.

"I'm glad to hear that."

"Can I tell you something? It's weird so don't judge me."

He nods.

"The night I showed up, looking for my passport, I tried to commit suicide, in this apartment. I had some pain pills and a bottle of water and I was going to take every last one of them. But," I stop.

"But what?"

"I heard music coming from the apartment to my left. It was a song by Kirk Franklin called *My World*

Needs You. That song kept playing over and over and God wouldn't allow me to finish, what I'd started.

So, I left here and went to see that chaplain, I met at the hospital, the time I burst my stitches. Turns out, she's Todd's mom. Anyway, I was too angry to hear what she had to say and that caused me to run, again. I ended up, at the airport, with a ticket to Jamaica. I don't know how long I'd been sitting there when Cam called about Brian dying.

Hearing that made me want to leave, even more so I showed up at your house. Upon leaving there, I came here to pack and when I asked security, about the neighbors, he told me there hadn't been neighbors in that apartment for weeks."

He's looking at me crazy.

"It's crazy, I know. I thought I was losing my mind."

"No Lyn, my facial expression isn't disbelief, if anything, it solidifies my faith."

"What do you mean?"

"When you left, I started praying for you. I know, you and I have never been big on church, but I started going, recently, with a coworker and I knew, that night I needed to pray for you." He steps closer to me. "Lyn, that night, it was God stopping you from doing something so final."

He grabs my hands. "Do you know how devastated we would have been to lose you? Babe, I know I hurt you and I'm sorry, but I love you. I love you with every fiber of me."

"I know Paul—" he kisses me.

I pull away when my cell phone rings. "That's probably security."

An hour and half later, my furniture has been delivered and set up.

"Paul, thank you again for doing this. I was going to ask one of the girls, but you happened to show up."

"No problem. I'm glad I could be here for you."

We walk to the door and it's awkward when we try to give each other a hug. Laughing, we take a step back.

"Will you allow me to take you to dinner?" he inquires. "Don't overthink it, it's just dinner as a way for us to start over. We have to start somewhere, right?"

"What about Kandis?"

"There's nothing going on between us. We're only co-parenting, for PJ."

I don't say anything.

"It's just dinner."

"Sure. Text me the place and time and I'll be there."

He smiles. "I'm going to get you to love me again Lyn, watch. Take care and lock up," he tells me, kissing me on the cheek.

When he leaves, I press my back against the door. "Lord, whatever your will is."

Kerri

The girls, along with Mike and I meet up for Bible Study at High Point. I wasn't sure if Shelby would make it, but she did, and I was happy to see her, out of the house. We make it to our seats, as soon as prayer is over.

"Good evening High Point. Isn't God good? Scratch that, isn't God better than good?"

"Yes ma'am, He is," I say with my hand in the air.

"I know, somebody here, yes, even here in this house of worship, is wiping your woes on your wrist of weakness. You're probably wrestling with wickedness and it feels like it's winning. You've wandered passed the warnings and now you're weighed down.

Somebody is looking at their wounds, that will not heal. You're questioning God about some mess, you got yourself in and you're tired. Well, High Point, God says He has the restoration, you've been seeking but you'll have to go through recovery.

Don't look at me like that. If alcoholics can have AA, drug addicts, gamblers and even sex addicts can have a place to go to recover; why can't Christians, for their spirituality? You do know that recovery means the act of getting something again that was lost, stolen or owed; right? See, you've been in that mess, so long that you've gotten comfortable.

You've been hateful for so long, that it's sucking the life out of those around you. Yes, I know you've tried to do it on your own, but it hasn't worked and today is your intervention, the start of a two-part series; recovery and restoration. Turn with me to Hosea 6:1.

It reads, *"Come, let us return to the LORD. For He has torn us, but He will heal us; He has wounded us, but He will bandage us."*

Today, people of God, you need help and the only way you can get the kind of help, you seek; you've got to return to God."

"How?" someone cries out. "How do we return to God, when it seems like He's the one causing us pain?"

Pastor Reeves pauses, smiles and then speaks. "By checking yourself into recovery."

"Like rehab?" someone else asks.

"Yes, in a sense but it's not a physical rehab. What I mean is, this work will all be inwardly or work that'll take place on the inside of you. Here's the bigger blessing, it's all covered, and you won't have to pay a dime or bill your insurance.

You won't have to pack a bag, but you will have to throw out some stuff. You won't have to change residence, but you may have to change who resides there. Are you ready to get started?"

"Yes," a few people say.

"Great then allow me to give you the list of God's custom-made treatment plans. These plans are for your good so that you can recover.

Detox program – *1 John 1:9, "If we confess our sins, he is faithful and just to forgive us our sins and to cleanse us from all unrighteousness." Psalm 51:10, "Create in me a clean heart, O God, and renew a right spirit within me."*

Individual therapy – *Matthew 6:6, "But when you pray, go into your room, close the door and pray to your Father, who is unseen. Then your Father, who sees what is done in secret, will reward you."*

Group Therapy – *Hebrews 10:25, "And let us not neglect our meeting together, as some people do, but encourage one another, especially now that the day of his return is drawing near."*

Christian based treatment – Bible Study, Sunday School, Worship Service and Prayer Meeting.

Everybody got those? If not, they'll be on the screen. Beloved, God's Recovery Program works and there's only one required book, it's called the Bible. There's no set time on your recovery because it's at your pace but you must have a wanting to be recovered and the faith that you will be.

You can start whenever you choose, all you have to do is write the date down and begin. Recovery works because I've tried it and I am not ashamed to tell it. I am a recovering addict of self-doubt, self-pity and no encouragement of self but I've been through recovery and I'm recovering.

Notice I didn't say recovered because every day is a struggle but if we stay in touch with our sponsor, God, He'll see us through the times we almost slip. Recovery is hard, but it can be done because after recovery, comes restoration."

"What's the difference?" I ask.

"Recovery is the action or process of regaining possession or control of something stolen or lost. Whereas restoration is the action of returning something to a former owner, place, or condition. Think of it like a building. You can't restore it, until you have possession, right? Well, the only way God can effectively restore you, you've got to come back to Him, through recovery."

"Wow," Ray says.

"We'll get into that, in the coming weeks," she tells us before continuing the study of the lesson.

Thirty minutes later, when she's done with the lesson, she says, "if there aren't any more questions, lets stand for prayer."

"Dear God, we thank you for what you've allowed to transpire in this place. God, we ask you, to forgive us for continually trying to do things on our own. We've tried everything and now God, give us the chance to try you. We're ready now, Father. Ready to return to you. We're ready to be recovered so that we can be restored.

And God, we know this process is going to hurt and we know it's going to take time but we're ready. Heal us, recover us, restore us so that we can be what you've created us to be. Now, as we leave this place but never your presence; allow us to make it home safely. Wrap us, in your arms so that those, who haven't had a good night's sleep, will get one tonight.

Keep us safe from hurt, harm and danger. Protect and provide for us. Thank you, God and amen. Go in peace until we meet again."

Chapter 6

Shelby

"Lord, thank you for keeping me another day and thank you for another taste of your grace. But God, I need you to help me. This has got to get better. Please Lord!" I say, wiping the tears when I wake up from a dream about Brian. I reach over and rub his side of the bed.

Even Brinae misses Brian because some nights, she cries herself to sleep and nothing I do can console her until I put a shirt, that smells like him, near her. My heart breaks for my baby girl. I roll over and look at the monitor to see she's still asleep, so I get up and shower, putting on something besides pajamas.

Sitting on the side of the bed, my cellphone rings.

"Hello."

"Shelby?"

"Yes."

"Hey, this is Derrick."

"Derrick, hey, how are you?"

"I hope you don't mind that I looked at your file, to get your number but I was worried about you. How are you?"

"I've been better," I sigh.

"Shelby, I'm so sorry to hear of Brian's passing. I've been out of the country, the last few weeks and got in last night. I was looking through my mail and saw the article about his death."

"Thank you. It's been hard but I'm doing my best to adjust," I answer in between a yawn.

"Are you sleeping?"

"When I can," I tell him.

"It doesn't sound like it's often. Shelby, I know how hard grief can be, but you have to take care of yourself and if you need something to help you sleep, let me know and I'll write you a prescription."

"I will."

"How is the baby? I know she's young, but your emotions still affect her."

"You know, that never dawned on me until these last few weeks. Some nights, she's okay but others, she cries until I put one of Brian's shirts under her. How does she know?"

"It's not uncommon for babies to grieve but they are so small and can't articulate it."

"What do I do, for her?"

"Cuddle with her more, try to keep things as normal

as possible, speak calmly when she's having one of those nights and keep providing his shirts."

"Thank you."

"You can also bathe her in some night time bath wash which will help relax her."

"Man, this is something new for the both of us, so we are learning together. Anyway, how was your trip? Was it a mission trip?" I ask, changing the subject.

"Yes, and it was great. We took some supplies over to Africa to help them stock a new children's hospital."

"You've always been great at that kind of work."

"I guess you can say it's my calling. Anyway. I have to get back to my rounds but Shelby, I'm here for you," he says as the doorbell rings. "When you're ready, let's do coffee or lunch."

"Thank you and I may just take you up on that. Call me next week and thank you for checking on me."

"Take care Shelby."

"You too," I say before hanging up and running to the door.

I open the door to find Brock, Brian's brother on my doorstep. "Aren't you a few weeks late?"

"I know and I'm sorry," he says reaching to give me a hug, but I step back.

"I'm so sick of hearing the word sorry, I could scream. What do you want?"

"I just want to talk," he says. "Please."

I step back to let him in.

"Shelby, I know I should have called—"

"No, you should have been here, a month ago when I was laying your brother to rest."

He sighs. "You're right. Regardless of the relationship between me and Brian, he was still my brother and I should have been here for you. Lately, this shit has been weighing heavily on me. He was all I had left."

"If Brian was all you had left, why wouldn't you respond the many times he reached out to you? You blamed him for your mom's death, a death caused by cancer. Oh, but you would call every time you needed something, though."

"I know you're upset, and you have every right to be, but I was dumb when our mom passed away. I took my anger out on Brian, because he was the oldest and I thought he could do anything. I didn't understand the circle of life and it left me angry at the world. That anger, it turned me to drugs and alcohol, but I got clean two years ago. When I met my wife, I called him, and we talked.

I apologized for all the things I'd said and done but I didn't ask him for forgiveness because I thought I'd have time to ask him, face to face. I was wrong," he says beginning to cry. "I didn't get to tell him goodbye."

I let him get his tears out.

"Are you done?"

"I was devastated when I heard Brian had died. I kept replaying your messages over and over, hoping it was a nightmare. I booked my plane ticket to come home but I couldn't bring myself to see him, in a casket because I knew how that affected me, when mom died. I was afraid of relapsing."

"Look Brock, I can't do anything about the past. Brian is gone and nothing either of us can do, will bring him back. I'm happy to hear that you've been sober and about finding a wife. However, it still doesn't explain why you're here."

"I don't need anything, from you Shelby, I promise. I only came to make sure you and the baby are okay and to see if there's anything I can do for you. My wife Jyema and I, will be here, for a few weeks because her job is thinking of transferring her back to Memphis. Here's my number," he says handing me a card. "It's my wife's card but I wrote it on the back."

I hear the baby crying. "I need to get her. Thanks for coming by and I'll call you. Maybe we can do dinner and I can meet your wife and you can get to know your niece."

"I'd like that."

"Great, I'll be in touch."

I walk him out and look at the card. "Lord, only with your permission will I let him in."

Lyn

I'm standing in front of the mirror, after getting dressed for dinner with Paul. I rub the scar on my neck and then I remember what Pastor Reeves said in bible study, in order to get to restoration, I've got to go through recovery.

"You can do this Lyn. It's only dinner."

I apply some lipstick and grab my things.

Thirty minutes later, I'm sitting outside of Ruth Chris. I take a deep breath and get out. I walk up to the hostess.

"Good evening ma'am, do you have a reservation?"

"Yes, it's under Paul Williams. I don't know if he's arrived yet?"

"Um, no ma'am, he hasn't but I can show you to your table."

"Thanks."

"Your server tonight will be Vincent and here are our specials."

A few minutes later, Vincent comes, and I order a glass of wine to knock the edge off. I pick up my phone to scroll through some new sites, for inventory to pass the time.

When Vincent returns with my wine, I ask for some time, to wait on Paul. I sip my wine and continue to scroll. After fifteen minutes and still no Paul, I start to get nervous.

Did I mix up the dates? No, I couldn't have because she had a reservation. Did I miss a call or text? No, my phone is in my hand.

I dial Paul's number. No answer.

I send a text.

ME: Hey, I'm at the restaurant.

Minutes pass, no response.

"Mrs. Williams, would you like me to put in an appetizer for you?"

"No thanks Vincent but I'd like order. I'll have this three-course special with the cucumber & tomato salad and crab cakes with creamed spinach."

"It also comes with strawberry shortcake for dessert, is that okay?"

"Perfect but can you make it to-go?"

"Sure thing."

I spend the next hour, enjoying my dinner while inwardly seething. Once I'm done, I pay my check and grab my dessert.

I was headed home but something told me, to go by Paul's house. I park and ring the doorbell.

"May I help you?" Kandis inquires, after opening the door.

"Wow," I laugh before turning to walk off.

"Lyn, Lyn; wait." Paul is yelling. "Wait, I can explain."

I keep walking.

By the time I get to the truck, he grabs my arm.

"Lyn, please let me explain. PJ got sick and we had to take him to Minor Med."

"And you couldn't pick up the phone?"

"I didn't—oh my God, dinner. Babe, I'm so sorry. Everything happened so fast and it slipped my mind."

"No, I slipped your mind. Got it."

I open my door.

"That's not what I meant," he sighs. "Just let me make it up to you."

"This was supposed to be you, making it up to me. You said, this was a starting point, in us starting over. We have to start somewhere, right? Those were your words, not mine. And to think, I really believed you, this time."

"I love you, Lyn."

"You may but it's evident, I'll always come last to them," I point towards the house. "Always."

"That's not true, you're the one I need. Just give me another chance."

"I'm done Paul."

"No," he says grabbing my arm, pulling me towards him. "No."

"Paul," Kandis says from the other side of the truck.

"Not now, Kandis."

"Did you tell Lyn, our news," she says with happiness falling from her lips.

"Kandis, go back in the house."

"We're pregnant, again," she says.

I look at Paul with tears in my eyes, "congratulations." I push him away and get in the truck, with him knocking on the window while she stands there and smile. I press the start button and for a split second, I want to run them both over but instead, I pull out the driveway.

"Got damn it," I hear him scream.

I walk into my apartment and as soon as the door slams, behind me, I scream.

"God, how much more must I suffer?"

I begin to pace in my living room, my phone constantly ringing over and over. I go back to the counter, get it and throw it into the wall.

"I'm tired," I cry. "I'm tired of hurting. You said you wanted me restored, is this how? I don't understand and I don't want to hear another freaking song. God, why are you punishing me?"

I slink down onto the couch. Then my anger rises, and I kick the coffee table over. The basket, on top, spills and I see the plane ticket, from a few weeks ago.

I pick it up.

A few minutes later, I have some clothes in a bag, my passport, purse and I'm pressing the down button for the elevator.

*****

"Good evening ma'am, how may I help you?"

"Good evening. I have an unused plane ticket that I'd like to exchange."

He takes it and types on his keyboard. "Yes ma'am, there'll be a change fee of 179 dollars."

"That's not a problem."

"When would you like to fly out?"

"The next available."

"Would you like to keep it as a one way?" he questions.

"Yes," I reply handing him my credit card.

"Very well. The next flight leaves at 5 AM."

"That works."

"Here's your card and your boarding pass. Thank you and enjoy your stay in Jamaica."

Chloe

"Hey, Mrs. French, how are you today?" Rita, the nurse in the NICU asks.

"I'm great but it's not Mrs. French. Please call me Chloe."

"I'm so sorry," she says. "I just assumed."

"It's okay. How is our feisty girl doing? I see that all of her tubes have been removed," I smile at Tamah as she stretches. "Is that a good thing?"

"That's because Dr. Conner is releasing her to go home today. According to her chart, she's passed all of her milestones and is currently weighing, four pounds and one ounce."

"Oh my God, you're coming home, my sweet girl!" I gush at her. "I'm so excited because I thought she was going to be released next week but this is perfect."

Rita smiles. "It's her feeding time, why don't you nurse while we wait for Dr. Conner. There's going to be a lot of information, to cover, so enjoy the quiet time with her."

I pick her up from the crib and move to the rocking chair. I get her comfortable on my breast and seeing her without, even the small tube of oxygen, is the most gratifying feeling.

I get my phone to Facetime Todd, who's in Gatlinburg.

"Hey daddy," I say when he answers, "look who I'm holding without all the tubes."

"She's off the tubes? Thank you, God."

"Yes, and she's coming home today. I'm just waiting for the doctor to come back around."

"That's great news babe. I'll be leaving here as soon as I am done with my last meeting, so I should be at your house, sometime tonight. Daddy will see you later, little girl."

"I will see you when you get here. Be careful, okay?"

"I will. See you tonight."

I hang up the phone and rub the sweetest thing God created. Tamah Denise French. I can't believe I'm someone's mom.

An hour later, Dr. Conner is tapping me on the arm. "Hey Chloe, I'm sorry to wake you."

"Dr. Conner, is everything okay with the baby?"

"Yes, everything is fine. As Rita told you, she's

been removed from all of the tubes. She's been eating great and she is up to four pounds. Her lungs are functioning great and she passed all the necessary tests. Chloe, your daughter is ready to go home."

"Oh Dr. Conner," I say throwing my arms around him. "That is great news. Will she be released today?"

"Yes, but it'll be a few hours as we go over all the necessary paperwork and answer any questions, you may have. I'll be around for a few more hours should you think of something. She's a very strong and blessed little girl."

"Thank you, Dr. Conner."

I text Todd, then I called the girls and Ms. Denise to let them know.

Four hours later, we're all packed up and ready to go. Pulling up, at home, I see all of the girl's cars, which makes me smile.

Kerri comes out, with a huge smile on her face.

"Don't you look pretty," I tell her. "You must have a date tonight." She doesn't say anything, before grabbing the baby and leaving me to get most of the things, by myself.

I shake my head.

Getting to the front door, all the girls are standing

there dressed in more casual clothes, than what I was expecting.

"What's going on?" I ask, looking at each one of them.

They ignore me and begin taking the stuff from my hands.

"Shelby? Ray? Cam? Kerri?"

"Shush woman and follow me," Shelby orders.

"But—"

She pushes me towards my bedroom and when the door opens, Tyra, my hairdresser and Monica, a makeup artist are waiting.

"What is this?" I inquire when I see a beautiful silk white maxi dress and shoes lying on the bed.

"Oh my God, what's happening?"

"Aht, aht; don't get all mushy. Go and take your shower so that you can get your hair and makeup done," Ray instructs from behind me.

"Ray—"

She only points to the bathroom.

After showering, getting my hair and makeup done, I get dressed. I must say this dress fits me perfectly. It's one shoulder, with the prettiest silver beading surrounding the top and matching shoes.

There's a knock on the door.

"Are you ready?" Shelby asks.

"Are you going to tell me what's going on?"

She shakes her head, no.

I roll my eyes.

"Are you ready?"

"Yes."

"Good, turn around."

She puts a blindfold, over my eyes. She grabs my arm, leading me, to what I think is the back door. When she removes the blindfold, I gasp at the sight before me.

My indoor patio has candles and lights everywhere. Curtains are hanging and tied back with silver ties.

"Oh my God," I cry with my hand to my mouth. Stepping out, I see Ms. Denise, Pastor Reeves, Mike, Cam, Thomas, Kerri, Lauren, Brittany, Ray and Todd holding Tamah.

"Todd," I exclaim. "What are you doing here?"

Denise takes the baby and he walks over to me, pulling me to the middle of the floor.

"You're in so much trouble," I say causing everybody to laugh.

"Chloe, I think everybody here knows how things started for us. It wasn't the best way, to begin things but I'd be lying if I say, I regret meeting you. From the short amount of time we've known each other, we've gone through a lot yet, we're here.

You've given me, the sweetest blessing, in my first daughter and another reason to smile. Chloe, I can't imagine living without you and our daughter. I want to wake up, to the both of you, every morning. I want you to get butterflies, in your stomach, when you see me because my eyes tell you, you're mine; only mine.

I want to watch Avenger and scary movies with you. I want to make memories and more babies, with you. I need to love you Chloe and that's why I'm asking you," he kneels, "to be my wife, tonight."

I look at the girls and they're all crying.

"Gul answer that mane," Cam says.

"Yes! Yes, Todd, I'll marry you but how can we do it tonight, with no marriage license?"

He stands and pulls me into a kiss.

"We can do that tomorrow, which will be our official wedding date but I'm making you my wife, in the eyesight of God, now."

We turn and Pastor Reeves, stands before us.

"Chloe, since Todd has already made his vow to you, is there anything you want to say?"

I take a breath. "God is amazing," I say as tears fall. "Todd, I had no intentions on meeting you, let alone marrying you but I'm so glad God's plan is much better than mine. You came into my life and in this short amount of time, you've opened up my heart to love again and you make it easy to love you. Well, when you stopped being a jackass."

Everybody laughs.

"You've given me a mom," I say looking at Denise, who is crying, "something I've never had, another sister and more than anything, you've made me a mom. Yes, our relationship isn't the ordinary, but I look forward to seeing where God takes us. From Avenger to scary movies, one more baby and plenty of memories; I'm here for it because I want to wake up to you in the mornings and lay down with you, at night."

"Todd and Chloe," Pastor Reeves says, "Bible says in 1 Corinthians 13: 4-7, *"Love is patient and kind. Love is not jealous or boastful or proud or rude. It does not demand its own way. It is not irritable, and it keeps no record of being wronged. It does not rejoice about injustice but rejoices whenever the truth wins out. Love never gives up, never loses faith, is always hopeful, and endures through every circumstance."*

Are you both willing to love one another?"

"Yes," we both say.

"Join hands. Todd, in taking your woman's hand, you are signifying that you have chosen her to be your lawful and wedded wife, forsaking all others. You are promising to love and cherish her, to honor and endure her, in sickness and in health, in poverty and in wealth, in the good that may lighten your ways and especially when bad may darken your days. Do you vow to be true to her in all these things until death shall part the two of you?"

"I do."

"Chloe, in taking your man's hand, you are signifying that you have chosen him to be your lawful and wedded husband, forsaking all others. You are promising to love and cherish him, to honor and endure him, in sickness and in health, in poverty and in wealth, in the good that may lighten your ways and especially when bad may darken your days. Do you vow to be true to him in all these things until death shall part the two of you?"

"I do."

"Are there rings?"

Todd hands them to her.

"Dear God, accept these rings as a symbol of love that shall never find an end. Bless these rings, by your power that as long as they adorn the fingers of Todd and Chloe that they will put you as the head. Guide them, instill in them and cover them with you.

Allow them to handle disagreements, according to your word and God, what you join together, don't let man, woman, neither child or foe put asunder. We thank you for the union and by your grace, may it always be blessed. Amen."

After exchanging rings, Pastor Reeves smiles, "By the power vested in me by the state of Tennessee, I now pronounce you husband and wife. Todd, you may kiss your bride."

"I cannot believe you pulled this off without me knowing," I say kissing him.

"He had a little help," Kerri says before they each give me a hug and she snaps a few pictures with her phone.

"Where's Lyn?"

"We don't know but I'm sure, she's okay. Tonight, this is about you and your new family."

"Chloe," Denise says, "I know we've only known each other a little while, but you make it so easy to love you and I'm honored to have you as a part of our family."

She wraps her arms around me and I cry. "Growing up without a mom, I didn't think I'd ever get to experience this."

"Well, you have me now."

Pastor Reeves walks up.

"Congratulations again," she says, giving each of us a hug.

"If it's okay, I'd like to seal tonight with prayer," Denise says.

I take Tamah from her and hold Todd's hand. Everybody surrounds us.

"Heavenly Father, we petition your throne, thanking you for restoration of life and love. God, you've allowed the manifestation of your power to reign, in the lives of Todd, Chloe and Tamah. At this moment, I ask you to bless their union. Bind the hand of the enemy so that nothing he tries, will prevail.

And as we surround them, in the physical, I ask that you surround them in the spirit, with angels of protection. Provide for them, cover them, comfort them and keep them. This we ask God, in your name. Amen."

"Amen."

Kerri

Walking into the bedroom, after showering, Mike is on his computer, in bed.

"Babe, have you ever thought about renewing our vows?"

He looks up at me. "No, have you?"

"Not until tonight. After we'd decorated Chloe's patio and I saw how happy she was, it got me to thinking. We've been through a lot, this past year and since our wedding anniversary is coming up, in August, I thought it would be a good idea."

"Boo, if that's what you want then let's make it happen."

I smile at him before sitting on the side of the bed to apply some shea butter to my feet.

"What do you think about Todd?"

"I like him. He seems like a cool dude and I saw the way he looks at Chloe. We spoke a little, while we waited on her to get home and he asked me to look over the plans for his new restaurant. He had a firm in Gatlinburg draw them up and he wants to make sure they're up to code for Memphis."

"That's good."

There are a few seconds of silence before he clears his throat.

"Did you know that coffee place, you liked is closed?" he asks, changing the subject.

"Which one?"

"The Coffee Spot," he says.

"Oh, yea, I know. Adrian told me."

"Adrian? Old dude, you used to mess with?"

"Yea, but it's not like that. He stopped by the bakery, a few weeks back and told me."

"Y'all still talk?"

"No." I finish putting my exfoliating socks on before sliding under the cover and turning off the lamp.

"Would you tell me if you were?"

"Yes, because I don't have anything to hide." I sit up and turn the light back on. "Mike, there's nothing going on between me and Adrian. What happened, before, was a mistake caused by wanting to fulfill fleshly desires and forgetting the problems we were having at home. It's over and will not happen again but if there's something you want to say or ask, do it so we can put this issue to rest."

"I'm not trying to argue about this, but I don't think

it's fair for you to be friends with a guy you slept with, that's all."

"We aren't arguing and him and I, aren't friends."

"Then why would he stop by to tell you about his place closing?"

"Because he'd been buying pastries, from me and he didn't want me to continue knowing they were closing."

"Really and you didn't think to tell me?"

"I didn't tell you because I didn't know. I knew somebody was buying a lot of pastries, on Mondays but not that it was him. He only told me, when he showed up."

I sigh. "Mike, there's nothing going on between us and we're not friends. As a matter of fact, I told him we couldn't be friends because it wouldn't be fair to you or his wife."

"Yet, he was buying from your bakery."

"Babe, I can't control that. Now, come on, this is crazy."

"It's not. Would you be okay with me being friends with someone I slept with?" he questions.

"Number one, I don't know who you slept with because I never asked and don't plan too. Number two, because of number one, I wouldn't know who you talk to and number three, I respect you enough; even through all we've endured to trust you. Shouldn't I get that same respect?"

"I do trust you."

"It doesn't sound like it."

"Ma," I hear MJ call out, on the baby monitor.

"I'm going to check on him."

"Kerri, I—"

"Forget it Mike."

I open my eyes to see Mike standing over me.

"Babe," he whispers, "come to bed."

I look around and realize, I'd fallen asleep next to MJ. I slowly slide out of his bed and tip toe out of the room.

I use the bathroom, wash my hands and get back into bed.

"Kerri, I'm sorry."

"Okay," I reply.

"I'm serious."

"I hear you Mike, but I hope we're not going to have this kind of problem, in our marriage, going forward. You have to trust me, enough, to know that I'd never break our vows again and if you don't then we need to reevaluate some things."

"You're right and I meant it, when I said it earlier. I trust you enough to believe you and I respect you enough to never, intentionally, break our vows again."

"Make me a promise. If there's anything you have doubts about or an issue with, you'll talk to me instead of jumping to conclusions."

"I promise. Will you promise the same thing?"

"I promise."

"Let's kiss so that we know it's real and by kissing, I mean the kind that ends with you on top of me," he winks.

"That I can do."

Ray

I'm working late, at the office, trying to get caught up on the notes from Anthony's meeting with Mr. Trapp.

I lay them on the desk and log into my Facebook account. I scroll through a few meme's and jokes. I click on the kid's pages, to be sure they aren't posting anything foolish. Refreshing the page, I see a post from Justin, made two hours ago.

"Sometimes, you have to tear away the version of you, made by people in order to embrace the you, you've been destined to be."

"Good for you," I say out loud as I continue scrolling. I stop when I see a post with Anthony and Kris' names tagged.

"When you say your prayers tonight, please whisper the name Kris Johnson. Anthony Johnson, keep your head up bro."

I click on the name, just to be sure it's the Anthony Johnson I know. When his page loads, I see the many posts. I grab my phone and dial his number. After a few rings, he answers with a groggy voice.

"Hey, did I wake you?"

"No," he sighs, "hold on."

It sounds like he's shuffling around.

"Ray?"

"I'm here."

"I've been meaning to call you but so much has happened since I left the office, a few hours ago. Kris tried to commit suicide. I found her when I got home."

My hand flies to my mouth. "Oh my God, Anthony, I'm so sorry. Is she going to be okay?"

"Right now, she isn't responding. The doctors have pumped her stomach and are trying different combinations of medicines but," he sighs. "I don't know how long she'd been like that."

"Oh my God. Where was your daughter?"

"She was at school. That's how I knew something was wrong because she didn't pick her up."

"What can I do?"

"I hate to ask this, but can you come and get Tori? She's been at the hospital with me, for a while and she's getting restless and Kris' parents won't be here until late tomorrow."

"Are you sure?"

"No, but I don't have anybody else to ask and I can't leave, right now." He says, sounding defeated.

"What hospital?"

"Methodist Germantown. I'll be in the ICU waiting room."

"I'm on my way."

I shut my computer down and grab my things.

"Anthony," I say touching his arm to wake him. He jumps causing Tori to wake up.

"Ray, thank you for coming."

"Ms. Ray," Tori yawns.

"Hey sweet girl, how are you?"

"Tired but daddy said we couldn't leave because mommy is sick."

"I know but that's why I'm here."

"You're taking me home?" she asks.

"Yes, I'm taking you home with me," I tell her. "Would you like that?"

"But I don't have any clothes."

"Maybe we can ask Ms. Ray to take you by the house to pack a small bag, would that help?"

I look at him.

"I know it's a lot to ask but I can give you the code to the garage and to the alarm. Tori can handle everything else."

"It's cool. Text me all the information. You ready?"

"Wait, did you read the notes from the meeting with Mr. Trapp?" he asks standing up.

I look at him, again.

"I need something to distract me, please."

"Yea, I looked at them but why are you even entertaining them again? I thought you'd already declined their original offer due to their bad debt and personality clash."

"I did but they've renegotiated the offer and I won't have to acquire their debt. They're going to file bankruptcy, so I'll only be, essentially, purchasing their customer list."

"I don't know. Let me look into it some more and then I'll give my opinion. Have you had Ross, from legal and Ontario from accounting take a look?"

"Yeah, they're looking over it now."

"Okay but in the meantime, is there anything else I can do, for you?"

"No, this is enough."

He grabs Tori. "You be a good girl for Ms. Ray, okay?"

"Okay daddy and kiss mommy for me."

"I will."

After getting Anthony's text, I take Tori home to get some clothes. She also grabs a stuffed animal, two books and some lip gloss. I make sure to get her toothbrush.

I stop and pick up some food before getting home, only to be met my Justin.

"Who is this?" he questions.

"What are you doing here?"

"JJ needed some stuff for a school project and I was dropping it off."

"Hi," Tori says to him.

"Hi," he replies, sticking out his hand. "I'm Justin."

"I'm Tori Johnson."

"Tori, can you go into the living room and I'll call you when it's time to eat."

"Yes ma'am," she runs off.

Justin laughs. "You're babysitting your boyfriend's kid now?"

"First of all, Anthony isn't my boyfriend. Second my business shouldn't be the business, you're minding, these days sweetie."

"All I did was ask a question."

"Question your mammy, not me. Hey, y'all come eat."

"Mom, is that Mr. Anthony's daughter?"

"Yea, that's Tori and she's spending the night because her mom is in the hospital and her grandparents won't make it here until tomorrow."

"Mommy is sick," she tells them.

"We know but she's going to be alright," Rashida tells her.

Justin touches my arm. "Can I speak to you?"

We walk into the living room.

"What's up?"

"I finally came clean to my mother."

"I saw your post, good for you but I'm surprised you're still alive. I thought she would have tied you up, in the basement to beat you straight."

"Really Raylan?"

I shrug.

"She actually took it better than I expected, actually. I've giving her some time to let it sink in and if she wants to be a part of our lives, she can be."

"Our?" I ask, looking confused.

"Mine and Garrett, my boyfriend."

"Wow," I laugh, "your boyfriend. That was fast."

"I'm sorry—"

"No, please don't apologize to me. Do you boo. Is

that it?"

"I'd like you and the kids to meet him."

"Meet who?"

"Garrett," he huffs.

"No."

"Raylan—"

"Justin, calling me by my name will not make me change my mind. We've been through this. I am not meeting your dude, period and stop asking."

I turn to walk off.

"JJ and Tristan want too."

I stop and turn back to him, squinting my eyes. "What?"

"I know you're mad but they're thirteen and fifteen, it's their choice."

"Listen, I can't stop them from being with you, meeting and spending time with your whomever and all that but what you do, stays outside of my house."

"Isn't that the pot, calling the kettle black."

"Excuse you?"

"You have your dude's little girl here, in front of them but you have an issue with them meeting my boyfriend."

I pinch the bridge of my nose and close my eyes,

counting to ten.

"I don't owe you an explanation on what the fuck I do, inside of 9099 Scottish Way, Memphis, TN 38125. If I want to have an orgy, in the living room, I can. If I want to walk around with my left titty nipple hanging out, I can. And if I choose to allow Anthony's daughter to spend the night, under my roof, while her mother fights for her life, I sho in the hell will. Now, why don't you skip your ass out of here."

"You know, I'm just about sick of you kicking me out of the house I help pay for, every time something is said you don't agree with. I have a right to be happy, just like you Ray. I don't deserve the way you treat me."

I walk pass him, into my bedroom then into the closet. I grab the big manila envelope and open it, snatching out the contents. I flip the pages until I get to the part I need. Stalking back down the hallway, I press them into his face.

"You see that? This says, this house belongs to me and I can care less how much you paid. It's mine now so don't let the door hit you, where Garrett sticks you, on your way out. Oh, and you can be happy with the scarecrow from the Wizard of Oz and I still wouldn't want to meet him."

I leave him standing there and go into the kitchen.

Chapter 7

Shelby

I'm in the kitchen, talking to the chef, I'd hired to prepare dinner for tonight. It's Valentine's Day and I asked the girls, with their significant others to dinner; along with Brock and Jyema.

I wanted to do this, as a way for them to see Brock, because it's been years since he's been home and for me to thank them for everything they've done, for me since Brian's death.

I head upstairs to get dressed, when the doorbell rings.

"Hey girl," I say to Ray, "you're early. Is everything okay?"

"Yea, Justin was at the house spending time with the kids and I needed to get out of there."

"Cool, I was headed upstairs to get dressed but there's some appetizers in the kitchen."

"Nah, I'll wait. Where's Brinae?"

"I put her down, about twenty minutes ago. She'll be up, soon because she hasn't been sleeping well, lately. I know it's because she misses Brian."

"I know she does, we all do, and you don't have to

be strong around us. We know you're mourning."

"I've leaned on you guys enough, these past two months. You all have lives too. Besides, I can't be anything, other than strong because I have the baby, Brian's company to run and finances to handle. I have too much to give up and Brian would never go for that."

"I hear you. When are you going into the office and do you need me to go with you?"

"No, I should be okay. I'm meeting with the accountant and lawyer tomorrow and the employees on next Wednesday. I don't foresee any major problems, though, but it will take some adjusting."

"Have you decided whether you're going to run the business?"

I shake my head no. "Real-estate will always be my baby and I have no plans to shut down the office, but I'm going to let Phillip handle the day to day operations, the accountant handle payroll and I'll do whatever else."

"It seems like you have it all figured out. I'm proud of you."

"I've had nothing but time to think about it and this takes my mind off of grieving." I tell her as the baby stirs, on the monitor.

"You go ahead and get dressed, I'll check on her," Ray tells me.

Ray is sitting on the side of the bed when I come out of the bathroom.

"Did I tell you, I talked to Derrick?"

"Dr. McHotty, no. Where has he been?" she asks, with a smile.

"He was on a mission trip to Africa. He wants to get together for lunch or coffee, soon."

"You should go because you need to get out of the house."

"Do I look that bad?" I laugh.

"Um, not today but child."

"Forget you, I've been out the house for church and bible study."

"That doesn't count."

"Don't you think it's too soon to be seen out with another man?"

"Another man who's your friend? Hell no."

"You know how people talk, Ray."

"Girl, f people and their thoughts and I mean the one with four letters and rhymes with yuck. Shelby, do what you need to do for your peace of mind and having friends, isn't a bad thing. Even if they happen to be of the male gender."

"I hear you."

The doorbell rings again.

"Can you get that while I put my hair up and check on the baby, again?"

"Sure."

"Thanks Ray."

A few minutes later, I come downstairs to Ray speaking to Brock and who I assume is his wife.

"Shelby," he says coming over to give me a hug. "This is my wife Jyema. Jay, this is my sister Shelby."

"Jyema, what a pretty name and it's nice to meet you."

"It's good to finally meet you too and my condolences on the passing of your husband. I wish we could have been here, but my husband is so dang stubborn," she rolls her eyes at Brock.

"Oh, don't I know because Brian was too." I tell her as Kerri and Mike come in.

"Hey everybody," they say.

I go over to hug them, making introductions.

"Guys, there's wine and liquor over on the bar and some appetizers set up in the kitchen. Please help yourself until dinner is served."

Kerri grabs mine and Ray's arm. "Hey, have you all heard from Lyn? I've been trying to reach her, but Jo says she hasn't been to the store in over a week."

"No, I've been so busy with trying to get Brian's affairs in order that I haven't had a chance to reach out to anybody, hardly."

"Me either," Ray adds, "but maybe Cam has—"

"Maybe Cam has what?" she inquires, walking in.

"Spoken to Lyn."

"Hold that thought," Cam says. "I know that ain't Brock."

"Yea."

"Girl, that boy done grewed the hell up."

"Did this fool just say grewed?" Ray asks as we laugh.

"Baby, I remember the last time he was here, and he didn't look nothing like that. Damn."

"Calm down Blanche from Golden Girls, that man is married."

"If that's his wife, beside him, I'll do her too."

"Girl, what happened to you turning over a new leaf?"

"I turned the mfer back. Y'all look, I've tried to make my marriage work. I promised Thomas I'd get help and

I have been. I've been doing counseling and I only did the counselor, once."

"Bitch," Ray shakes her head.

"What? Hell, I had to take baby steps. Anyway, after him and one time, with the prosecutor; I cut everybody off and started taking therapy seriously. You know what that got me?

A dry coochie and the 3rd degree from Thomas every time he sees me talking to a man. I'm sorry y'all but if this is the way life is going to be, I may as well cheat. At least, I'd be happy."

"Wait, you ain't had no sex from Thomas?" Ray and I both ask, at the same time, whispering.

"Once and it was a wham bam, thank you ma'am; on his part, not mine," she's saying when Thomas walks in. "Ugh, here his judgmental ass come."

We all try to keep from laughing.

"Shelby, Ray and Kerri, it's nice to see you ladies. Happy Valentine's Day."

"Hey Thomas and Happy Valentine's Day to you. There's liquor on the bar and appetizers in the kitchen. I'll be right back."

Cam

I follow Shelby into the kitchen. "Shelby—what the hell? Chelle?"

"Hi," she smiles. "I didn't know you were going to be here."

"Damn, I almost didn't recognize you with clothes on. How have you been?"

"Great, actually. I'm a full-time chef now and business has been great," she beams.

"I bet."

"No," she laughs, "not like that. I don't do that anymore. I have an investor who helped me start my business, so I wouldn't have to do that part of it."

"That's great. Well, the food smells great and you look good."

I grab Shelby's arm, pulling her out of the kitchen.

"How in the fuck did you find her, out of all the chefs in Memphis?"

"You shared her information on Facebook and since you don't post regularly, when I went to your page and saw that she was running a Valentine special, I booked her. What's the big deal?"

"She's the one Thomas and I had a threesome with?"

My mouth falls open. "Are you serious?"

"What are y'all whispering about?" Thomas asks, walking up on our conversation.

"Shelby's choice of chefs, for the night. Why don't you go and see who it is?"

When he walks around the corner, she and I burst into laughter when Chloe, Todd and the baby come in.

"Girl, you're going to hell," she tells me, and I shrug.

I let her go and walk into the kitchen. Thomas abruptly stops talking.

"Uh, what's going on?" I ask looking from him to her. "Why did you stop talking?"

"I didn't. We were talking about the menu and Valentine's Day."

"Oh, is that all because it looks like I intervened on a personal conversation. Is there something I'm missing?"

"Camille, don't start anything because there's nothing going on." Thomas says huffing like I'm getting on his nerves.

"Hold on because—"

"Everybody is here so we can eat," I hear Shelby say.

"Let's eat," he says turning me around and leading me to the dining room.

"What's going on with you and her?"

"Nothing."

"Nigga, if you think for a moment, I believe that, you're crazy. Don't worry though, I won't say anything tonight, but I will find out."

Once we're seated at the table, Shelby stands at the head.

"Okay, I'm going to try to get through this without crying." She takes a deep breath. "The last year has been draining, hurtful, mind blowing and hard. Never would I have imagined our lives being like this. Yet, I've come to realize the true meaning of, life is but a vapor. I understand it more than I ever thought I would.

That is why, I decided to have this dinner tonight. First, to welcome Brock and Jyema home. They'll be moving back to Memphis, permanently as she is the new VP of Ceva Logistics Memphis branch."

Everybody stops to congratulate them.

"Secondly, I wanted to take this time to personally thank each of you. You all have been my front, back and sides and without you, I don't know how I would have made it, these last two months. I am thankful that God has surrounded me with a village of sisters and brothers who love me. Okay, I'm going to stop. Can someone say grace?"

Brock stands. "God, we thank you for the food we are about to receive. I ask, God, that you'd bless it and remove anything that may cause us harm. Bless the hands of the cook and then God, bless those who sit around this table. Death may have bought us all together yet we're thankful that death cannot keep us apart. Thank you God and we ask that you continue to watch over us. Amen."

"Amen."

Chelle comes out and begins serving the table.

"Where's Lyn," Chloe asks.

"I don't know," Kerri answers. "I told Shelby and Ray that I've been trying to reach her."

"She's in Jamaica," I tell them.

"Jamaica?" we all say at the same time.

"Kelsey didn't tell me she was gone, out of the country," Kerri states.

"Kelsey probably doesn't know or care. Lyn has been there, about two weeks now. I thought she would have reached out to y'all," I say picking up a shrimp.

"Why is she in Jamaica Cam, what happened?"

"That motherfucking Paul is what happened," I say. "Him and Lyn were supposed to go out to dinner, his idea, as a way of starting over but he stood her up. She goes by the house and Kandis is there who couldn't wait to tell Lyn their great news. She's pregnant again, by Paul."

"Oh my God," Shelby drags out, "is she okay?"

"As well as to be expected, seeing her husband has been lying and making promises about wanting them to be restored and starting over," I remark, throwing down the end of the shrimp. "But I guess, he's full of it, too."

Thomas cuts his eye at and I roll mine, at him.

"Did she say how long she's going to be gone?" Chloe inquires.

"No. She has Jo taking care of the store and she gave me access to check on her apartment. Hell, if I were her, I wouldn't be in a hurry to come back. What does she have to look forward to other than a lying, sack of shit for a husband? I sweatergawd," I say sounding it out just like that, "I want to knock his freaking head in for hurting her, again. Y'all, if Lyn hurts herself over Paul's, Shrek looking ass, I'm going to jail for murder."

"Calm down Bonnie," Kerri says.

Chelle comes back to take the appetizer plates.

"I'm seriously worried about her. Hell, I know how she feels and not having someone, in your corner, who said they would be there, it hurts worse than any physical pain."

"Lyn wouldn't hurt herself, would she?"

"Yes," Mike says. "I don't know everything that's going on with Lyn, but I know how it feels to be in a dark and desolate spot, feeling like you have nothing else. She's more than likely at her breaking point and when you get there, you do one of two things. You either, get help and recover or you spiral. I know."

"What do we do?"

No one answers while Cher places the plates of salmon, fingerling potatoes, baby carrots and asparagus. When she's done, Mike continues.

"Offer your help. Even when she refuses it, keep offering. When she doesn't answer, keep calling and if she isn't home, in a soon, go get her."

"Great advice, Mike, thank you." I tell him.

"I've been where she is and the one of the things

that helped me stay in rehab was knowing my wife was there, waiting."

"Aw, that's sweet," I add, "to have a spouse who is there and willing to actually forgive, like they say instead of constantly throwing your mistakes, in your face. Must be nice."

Thomas looks at me and again I roll my eyes.

Ray

"What do we do, to help her."

"I agree with Mike," Brock adds. "I'd been an addict for years, doing any and everything you could think of. I thought nobody cared about me even though Brian would call and leave messages. Sometimes more than one a day and although I rarely returned them, he'd keep calling.

I'd say he was crazy but in hindsight, he was keeping me connected because had I lost that connection, I probably would have succeeded with the suicide attempts, I thought about. I didn't realize what he was doing, when I was incapacitated, from drugs and alcohol but going to rehab, taught me that.

Each time the phone rang, I got a voicemail or text; he was keeping me connected, letting me know he was there." He pauses when tears begin to run down his face. "I'm sorry," he says, "but you all have to keep her connected. It might not save her, but she'll know you care. Let her know she has someone waiting. I had this beautiful woman who I made my wife. My only regret, not telling my brother how much he helped me."

He covers his face with the napkin and cries.

Shelby gets up and goes over to him.

"Brock, your brother knew you loved him. He only gave you the time and space, you needed but he knew. And you didn't have to ask him, for forgiveness because he'd already given it."

"Whew," I say dabbing my eyes. "That connection Brock speaks of, is real. When you've been through storm after storm, those silent moments can be rough. It seems like those are the moments the enemy waits on, to pounce you like prey.

I mean, you can be the strongest, among your friends and family but when you're all by yourself with nothing to drown out your thoughts, yeah," I pause, "you have to stay connected. I thank God for you girls because you've kept me connected plenty of times, without even knowing it."

"Okay," Shelby says, wiping her face. "This isn't how I'd planned for dinner to go but I'm glad we can be open and honest with one another. I know we have our food, in front of us but if you don't mind, can I say a quick prayer for Lyn?"

"Yea, of course, sure;" everybody says.

We all grab hands.

"God, you're all knowing and all powerful and this is why, we come to you; tonight. God, watch over our sister, Lyn, wherever she may be. Keep her safe, not only physically but mentally. God, we don't know what all she's enduring, what she's had to face and the pain she feels but you do.

We don't know what she's hearing, in those silent moments or the thoughts she's having but this is why, we're coming before you, in the midst of dinner to ask of you. Surround her with angels, who will protect her. Give her peace, in this storm and let her know it won't always be like this.

Then God, let her know that we're praying for her. Every time she sees a call, let her feel our presence with her until she's ready to answer. Each time she feels like she can't go on, put it on us to call her so that we can keep her connected. Father, will you please do that, for her and for us because we don't know if we can handle another loss, right now. And while you're listening, bless those gathered around this table.

May we always find love, peace, forgiveness, comfort and understanding among us. May there always be a table to gather around, a conversation to be had, food to eat, love to give, a shoulder to cry on, arms to hug and a friend to lean on.

May those who need help, get it and those who've had help, offer it. Bless every family and every person. Don't let us perish alone, in our thoughts but give us strength to ask for the help we need. Thank you, Father, for family and for peace. We love and thank you, father. Amen."

"Amen."

"Does anybody need their food warmed?"

"Nah, we're good."

"Brock," Cam says, "how does it feel to be home?"

"Great actually. I didn't know how things would be, once we got here but I'm glad we came because I miss things like this."

"Do you all have any children?" I question.

"Not yet," Jyema answers. "We wanted to spend time getting to know us, as a couple first while we established our lives."

"That's a great idea because child, marrying the wrong person can lead to some hellish days and nights." Thomas says causing everybody to look at him.

"He's speaking from experience." Cam says before laughing.

"Chloe and Todd, when is the honeymoon?" Shelby asks to break the tension. They both look at each other.

"We are thinking of Maui, in August."

"Wait," Kerri says, swallowing her food. "Mike and I are thinking of renewing our vows, in August."

"Then let's make it a family trip, do you mind?" Chloe asks Todd who shakes his head no. "I've been doing some research and it says August is great there. Plus, the baby will be eight months and should be okay to travel. Speaking of baby, don't y'all forget that she's being Christened, in two weeks, after bible study." Chloe says, excusing herself to check on the baby.

"Todd, how are you liking fatherhood?" Mike asks him as we continue to eat.

"It's amazing. Tamah is healthy and is doing great. It's us, who's not okay," he laughs. "I didn't know how hard it is having a newborn who's been in the NICU, for over two months. She's still on their schedule and it's taking some getting used too. Chloe has been handling it, but I know she's tired."

"It'll get better once she adjusts to being home."

"How is it being newly married?" Shelby asks.

"You know, it's better than I could have expected. Chloe is amazing."

"Dude, bump that," Cam says. "Have you all broke that bed in, since y'all are married and er'thang?"

"The bed, the kitchen sink, the patio—you name it." Chloe says, walking in as Todd's face is beat red.

"That's what I'm talking about," Cam jumps up and gives her a high-five. At least somebody, is getting sex on the regular."

Chloe

When we make it home, Todd is still laughing about Cam. We walk into the nursery to get the baby ready for bed.

"Do y'all always talk like that?" he questions

"Babe, Camille is the life of any party and her mouth has no filter but yeah, we do. We've known each other for a long time and it's always been that way."

"I'm glad you have them to lean on."

"Yea, I just wish Lyn was there."

"Have you thought about calling her?" he asks. "I'm sure she'd love to hear your voice."

"I haven't but that's a good idea. I'll call once I get the baby down because Cam gave us her phone number. Can you turn the water on, in the sink so it can warm up?"

After bathing, nursing and burping Tamah, I lay her down. I go back into the living room and grab my phone. I dial the number to the resort, Cam gave me. She said Lyn didn't have her phone, but I could be transferred to her room.

"Sandals Resort, Montego Bay, how may I help

you?"

"Yes, can you transfer me to the room of Lynesha Williams, please?" I ask before spelling her name.

"One moment."

The phone rings a few times before it gives you an option to leave a message.

"Hey Lyn, this is Chloe. I hope you don't mind but Cam gave me your contact information. How are you enjoying Jamaica? Has it been everything you need? I pray it has but I want you to know that you are loved and missed. Hurry home because your niece is waiting for you. Oh, she's going to be Christened on the 27th, after bible study and I hope you can make it. Love you."

I release the call and say a quick prayer. Walking into the bedroom, there's music playing and the only light, is coming from the open blinds and some candles placed on the nightstands and dresser.

"Babe, what's this?" I inquire, laying my phone down.

"Our wedding night, do over."

Todd pulls me into him and we begin to dance. I close my eyes, listening to the words of the song playing.

"I said never again, been down this road before.

Then you showed me my best friend, could be something and more. Still, I chose to ignore when you kept showing me the truth. And if what this is, is loving, all I'll ask of you… just give me 'til two thousand and sixty-four. That is all I need."

"What song is this?"

"It's called 'Twenty Sixty-Four' by Avery Sunshine."

"How did you find it?"

"I know you like to listen to music, so I went to YouTube. I've heard Avery Sunshine before, so I searched her name and this album came up and I think, this song, defines us perfectly."

"How so?"

"She swore she'd never get married again but she said one day, he called and told her, they were going to get married. When he did, she said she knew it was love because it felt right. She prayed and said, if love feels like what she's found, then all she wants is for God to give her until two thousand and sixty-four, with him."

"Wow," I say, tears filling my eyes.

"Will you give me that Chloe French?"

I look at him, with tears streaming before passionately kissing him, like it's the first time and we'd been waiting a while.

When we pull away, we stare at each other.

"I love you, Chloe."

"I love you too and I plan to give you every second that God gives me."

We continue to slow dance until the song goes off. When it does, 'Boo'd Up,' by Ella Mai plays.

"Really?" I laugh.

"I like her," he says before we begin to dance together, and I start singing along with her.

"Feeling, like I'm touching the ceiling, when I'm with you I can't breathe. Boy, you do something to me."

He smiles, and we continue to dance before I put my arms around his neck, while grinding and singing to him, *"Listen, my to heart go ba-dum, boo'd up, biddy-da-dum, boo'd up. Hear my heart go ba-dum, boo'd up."*

I grab his hand and lead him to the bed.

Pushing him back, I begin to undress and when I get ready to lay on top of him, the baby cries.

I drop my head onto his chest and we both laugh.

Lyn

I'm sitting on the beach, looking out at the water. There are families, all around me with kids laughing and parents who look like they love each other.

I'm looking down at this journal, that I purchased and picking up the pen, I begin to write.

Dear Lyn,

If I could go back and tell my eighteen-year-old self anything, it would be … this journey is going to hurt like hell but you're stronger than you think you are. If I had the chance to revisit that Lyn, the one who thought the world would be easy, I'd tell her … there's going to be some rough spots but you're stronger than you think you are.

Girl, you're going to face some heartache and pain but you're stronger than you think you are. You're going to be victimized and left with nightmares and scars, but you're stronger than you think you are. You're going to make mistakes, a lot of them, but you're stronger than you think you are, and you'll survive them.

Lyn girl, I wish I could tell you that our marriage

was built to last but it isn't and yet, we're still stronger than we think and can survive.

I put down the pen for a moment, wiping the tears that were wetting up the paper.

Life is hard, it's going to get ugly and sometimes you'll feel as if there isn't anything to look forward too but then God reminds us, if I didn't need us, I wouldn't continually give us breath, blessings and grace.

Yes, we've experienced a lot, some good and some bad; but we're making it. Lyn, we're making it. You just have to make it through.

Signed,

Lynesha Williams

2/24/19

I pick up my shoes and head towards the hotel.

When I get to my room, I see the light flashing on the phone. Each time it has rung, over the past weeks, I've let it go to the voicemail. Today will be the first time I've checked it. I press the speaker button, then the message icon.

"You have six new messages."

I sigh as the first one begins.

"What's up trick? Look, I know you're probably out

getting sand in the crevice of your bootie, but I wanted to let you know, I'm thinking about you. Oh, and I gave your contact number to all the girls, so expect them to call. Okay bye, I love you. Call me."

I shake my head at Cam's message before laughing while deleting it.

"Message two."

"Hey Lyn, this is Chloe. I hope you don't mind but Cam gave me your contact information. How are you enjoying Jamaica? Has it been everything you need? I pray it has but I want you to know that you are loved and missed. Hurry home because your niece is waiting for you. Oh, she's going to be Christened on the 27th, after bible study and I hope you can make it. Love you."

"Message three."

"Hey Lyn, it's Shelby. I know you've been going through some things and needed this time away but don't stay gone too long. We need you; we miss you and more than anything, we love you. Come home soon but if you still need time, call and we'll come to you."

"Message four."

"Lynesha Williams, I can't believe it's been almost three weeks since I've heard your voice. In case you've forgotten mine, it's Ray. I miss you," she fake cries. "Hurry home so we can love on you and hear about all the stuff you've done. Wait, you better be enjoying that beautiful place. If not, I'm kicking your ass. Anyway, love you and come home."

"Message five."

"It's me, Cam, again. I didn't want nothing, just letting you know that I'm not going anywhere and if you haven't gotten your ass back to the state of Tennessee and the city of Memphis, in the next few days, I'LL FIND YOU," she says in a creepy voice. "Cam out."

"This girl is crazy," I laugh.

"Message six."

"Lyn, hey it's Kerri. I miss you," she sings, "and I have no one to taste my new recipes. I love you and I'm missing you something terrible."

I sit on the bed, for a few minutes before I undress and get in the shower. When I'm done, I get out and wipe the mirror off. I run my hand across the scar on my neck.

"You can cover it up Lyn, but it'll still be there."

I wrap the towel around me before going out, throwing on a maxi dress, some flip flops, getting the key to the room and going downstairs.

Inside the hotel's business center, I log into American Airlines and book my flight home, for the next morning.

Chapter 8

Pastor Reeves

"Good evening High Point," I say after prayer. "Isn't God good? Scratch that, isn't God better than good?"

"Yes, He is."

"All the time."

"Amen."

"A few weeks ago, we spoke on the subject of recovery. If you remember, I gave you four types of therapy as part of your recovery program. Recovery as in rehab. High Point, I've told you this, but God says, He has the restoration, we've been seeking but we'll have to go through recovery before we get to restoration.

See, I figure if there can be rehab for the physical, surely there can be rehab for the spiritual. Rehab, which is to rehabilitate or restore. If you missed that particular study, of God's custom treatment plans, they'll be on the screens and Deacon Strong has some printouts.

I will not go through each one, of them tonight, but God's custom-made treatment plans are for your good so that you can recover. What does God offer? Well, a detox program, from *1 John 1:9* and *Psalm 51:10*. Individual therapy, from *Matthew 6:6*. Group Therapy from *Hebrews 10:25* and finally Christian based treatment; such as Bible Study, Sunday School, Worship Service and Prayer Meeting.

Understand, not everybody will go through the stages of recovery and restoration, at the same time. Truth is, it may even take more than one go, at recovery before we even make it to restoration and that's okay. There is no limit on the amount of time, it takes for you to be recovered and/or restored.

Here's the good news, God doesn't hold it against you. All God wants is us recovering and restored. God doesn't keep count. I don't know about you but that's good news to a sinner like me. One who sometimes, still find herself, in the mess of life. One who still sometimes, make mistakes and one who has to call on her sponsor for guidance.

God doesn't keep track of our faults and He doesn't hold the many times; we need rehab against us. I thought I'd repeat that, for someone under the sound of my voice. The believer who got up this morning, still toiling with some stuff the altar prayer didn't loose you from. I'm speaking to the believer, who finds yourself in the dark place and no amount of scripture can get you out of.

I'm speaking to the believer who keeps crying out to a silent God. I came tonight, in beast mode, for the one, three, fifteen or thirty of you who after you've laid out on your face, your calls to God are still unanswered. Your fast is over and you're still no clearer on the situation at hand. Truth is, you truly believe God has forsaken you.

I got good news, tonight High Point and it's right here in the word. Turn with me to Amos, chapter nine. Whew Jesus," I exclaim, speaking in tongue. "This word is good tonight. In Amos, nine starting at verse eleven, the word says; now this is after the chapters of judgment and Israel's inability to learn and an unanswered call to repentance.

The word says, "*In that day I will restore the fallen house of David. I will repair its damaged walls. From the ruins I will rebuild it and restore its former glory. And Israel will possess what is left of Edom and all the nations I have called to be mine.*" The Lord has spoken, and he will do these things. "*The time will come,*" says the Lord, "*when the grain and grapes will grow faster than they can be harvested.*

Then the terraced vineyards on the hills of Israel will drip with sweet wine! I will bring my exiled people of Israel back from distant lands, and they will rebuild their ruined cities and live in them again. They will plant vineyards and gardens; they will eat their crops and drink their wine. I will firmly plant them there in their own land. They will never again be uprooted from the land I have given them," says the Lord your God."

God says, in that day. What day, the day He shall restore you. Restore, the action of returning something to a former owner, place, or condition. Let me explain something, because maybe you aren't understanding why I feel the need to run around this building. We look at the situations, we must face, and want to curse God. We complain about the moments, things break us but how can God restore what ain't been broken?

Oh, I know it doesn't feel good but when has been broken ever felt good? Yet, brokenness leads us to recovery then restoration. And if God is dealing with you, at this very moment, it's because there's something broke; within you that needs His attention.

His attention because He's the manufacturer and creator who owns the parts needed to restore you back to wholeness. Stop fighting Him, stop forsaking Him, stop ignoring Him, stop fighting Him and let Him restore what He created.

Let God repair that heart filled with holes from brokenness, your spirit that's filled with leaks from mess, your lungs that aren't functioning properly because you're breathing in the wrong stuff, your blood filled with hater toxins because you're around the wrong folk, your veins that are clogged with anger and your joints that are locked from non-movement. Beloved, you need restoration."

"You talking good Pastor," some yells out.

"What are you willing to sacrifice to get the restoration you need?"

"Jesus," someone calls out.

"Are you willing to sacrifice you? Are you willing to give God you, if it means Him restoring you? Are you willing to give God all of you, if it means Him making you whole? Understand, people of God, this recovery and restoration will not stop you from going through various trials, that's a part of the journey; yet, it allows you to know that even after everything I might endure, I can be restored.

The greatest part, God still blesses. When we're in rehab the first, fifth or fiftieth time, God still blesses.

When we're in the midst of restoration, God still blesses. Please don't think for one moment, God can't bless us when we're broken. Baby, being broken in God is the blessing.

Anybody willing? For my Bible tells me in Micah 7:8-11, *"Do not rejoice over me, O my enemy. Though I fall I will rise; Though I dwell in darkness, the LORD is a light for me. I will bear the indignation of the LORD Because I have sinned against Him, Until He pleads my case and executes justice for me.*

He will bring me out to the light, And I will see His righteousness. Then my enemy will see, and shame will cover her who said to me, "Where is the LORD your God?" My eyes will look on her; At that time, she will be trampled down like mire of the streets. It will be a day for building your walls. On that day will your boundary be extended."

Anybody ready to be restored?"

I call for an altar call as the musician begins to sing, 'Way maker.'

"You are here, moving in our midst. I worship you; I worship you. You are here, working in this place. I worship you; I worship you. Way maker, miracle worker, promise keeper, light in the darkness; my God,

that is who you are."

"Dear God, thank you for what you've allowed to happen in this place. Tonight, oh God, I ask that you meet us at this altar, restoring every person who had the courage to make their way. Father, they're in need of restoration. Father, they are in need of you. Have your way. You don't need my permission, to move me out of the way. Walk through this altar and restore."

I begin to speak in tongue as I walk from person to person, praying. It takes over thirty minutes, but it was worth it. I kneel at the altar, for a few minutes, in communion with God before I have to go back to dismiss bible study and prepare for the dedication of Baby Tamah.

Chloe

Most of us are crying and trying to get ourselves together, after that bible study, especially after seeing Lyn.

When Pastor Reeves opened the altar and I saw her go and kneel, I gave Todd the baby and joined her, followed by the rest of the ladies.

Mama Denise began to pray over her and she lost it, right there. She began to cry out and the first time, she spoke in tongue.

Once we could finally move, we all surround her.

"Lyn, we are so happy to see you."

After dismissal of Bible study, we make our way to the front of the church. Todd is still holding the baby, who is actually awake.

This time, we are surrounded by family.

Mama Denise, Taya and all the ladies, their children and spouses. I've already started to cry.

Pastor Magnolia opens a book and begins to read, "We know, it is because of God, that we've been given this little girl, who is before me. Therefore, we stand, tonight before His throne and an open heaven, dedicating her back to Him. In humble submission, we commit, before God and those in attendance to teach, baby Tamah, what it means to live in faith and from the Word of God. We stand, tonight on our own accord, vowing to share with other believers, our commitment to parenting this child in a godly manner."

When she's done, I raise the piece of paper and begin to read. "We desire for our child to be faithful to Christ, the church, and his family. Our desire, for Tamah Denise, is to live by faith and for God to make her courageous, kindhearted, and gentle. We commit to raising her in a way that glorifies Jesus, while giving her room to be who God has destined her to be. May she always find God, know God and love God."

I take the baby from Todd who speaks next. "Our prayer, for Tamah Denise, is that she may be a well of righteousness for all who cross her path. We pray that she will love by the same love God has given her. We pray she will always know her worth and never be embarrassed to walk in her purpose. We further pray that we shall see all the blessings she will birth. We know that God has everything planned, according to His will and that is why, He allowed her to grace this world, before her scheduled time. We, also pray, that she will fall so in love with Jesus that she'll never give up and never, ever lose hope."

Shelby goes next, "My prayer for Tamah Denise is power. Power to walk into places, God has ordained for her life. Power to speak with authority and command, everything she's due. Power to be recovered and restored."

Cam speaks. "My prayer for Tamah Denise is mercy. May she always pull from a never-ending flow of mercy to forgive others. May she be filled with mercy to find compassion for those who will make mistakes, break promises and who might even hurt her. May she always have mercy to offer grace."

Kerri lets out a breath as she dabs her eyes with tissue. "My prayer for Tamah Denise is patience. May she always have patience to endure, to forgive and to wait."

Ray pauses before speaking. "My prayer for Tamah Denise is understanding. May she always find understanding, in every situation and not judgment. May she be capable of offering sympathy, when it's required, compassion when it's called for, insight when it's due and discernment at all times."

Taya goes next. "My prayer for Tamah Denise is wisdom. May God fill her with wisdom to seek Him, know Him, love Him, honor Him and obey Him. May this wisdom be the key to opening doors, no man can shut. May this wisdom be her guide, forever."

"My prayer for Tamah Denise is peace," Lyn says as tears fall. "May she be given peace from the generational curses of her bloodline. May the peace of God, be so heavy, within her that she never knows what it feels like to be broken and rejected. May God's peace allow her to survive, with strength like that of Sampson. Tamah Denise, may God's wisdom, peace, patience, understanding, mercy and power be your portion; all the days of your life."

Mama Denise speaks, "Tamah Denise, God has seen fit to bless you with six aunts who will love and cover you, by God's power. My prayer for you, little girl, is for you to always know that grandma will be right here, for you. I'll pray, love, spoil and raise you to the best of my ability until my dying day."

By the time they are done, I am a sobbing mess. Todd had to take the baby from my arms.

"Amen," we all say.

"Let us pray," Pastor says. "Our Father, as we

stand, in your anointing, we first ask for your forgiveness. Search us, God and remove anything within us, that will not allow us to hold up the vows we made known to you. While you're removing, forgive us. Forgive us so that we can be closer to you.

Then God, we thank you for a blessing, who couldn't wait to get to earth. Thank you for the smallest blessing, you've allowed to grow, in our presence. More than anything God, we thank you for the restoration, healing and deliverance of her family. It is because of you, God, that we are able to stand tonight, in fellowship and unity, dedicating Baby Tamah to you.

We know the hardness of life's journey, but I believe, you've surrounded her with the right witnesses, who will ensure she makes it. Now God, wash us in your blood, cover us by your love and surround us with your angels. You've created this baby and you gave her, as a blessing, to the parents she deserves.

Give us, as the village, the provisions to teach her according to your word. For the Bible tells us in Mark nine and forty-two, "*whoever causes one of these little ones, who believe in you, to sin; it would be better for him to tie a millstone around his neck and be thrown into the sea."* God, we vow to do right by this child and we thank you for entrusting her to us. If you believe, say amen."

"Amen."

Cam

I'm changing the sheets on our bed.

"What's up Thomas?" I ask without turning around.

"How did you know I was standing here?"

"Because I smell your cologne. Did you just put some on?"

"No," he stutters.

"Hmm, okay."

"What's going on?" he questions.

"With?"

"Us," he says coming in and closing the door before helping to pull the comforter on his side.

"Oh, there's a us? Hmm, that's news to me because I didn't know."

"Camille, I'm sorry but I've been trying to figure things out between us."

"How's that working for you because it's surely not working for me. Thomas, it's been months since everything happened and you're still treating me like a stranger. You asked me to move back into our bedroom and for what, when you still haven't touched me."

"That's the problem, everything with you is always

about sex, Camille."

I let out a long sigh. "Okay."

"Okay what?"

"Okay, I'm done with this shit! I'm done apologizing, I'm done explaining myself and I'm done being treated like my feelings don't matter. Yes, I messed up, but you said you'd forgiven me. I go to that freaking therapy, when I don't want too but I do, for you. I'm here, every got damn day and night and it's still not enough."

"You're going to far because I have forgiven you."

"That's bullshit because this isn't forgiveness, Thomas. What else do you want from me? Should I get a chastity belt, would that make you trust me? Or are you turned off by me?"

"No, that's not it."

"Then what is it? Are you no longer in love with me?"

"Yes, I'm in love with you, Camille but I don't know how to make you happy. I don't know how to measure up to everything you desire." He states, grabbing a pillow. "Each time I think I'm ready to be with you, intimately again, I think about all the people you've probably slept with and I can't get pass it."

"Thomas, you are what I desire."

"Then why were you cheating?"

"Because you allow it."

"What?" he says, stopping mid fluff of the pillow.

"Thomas, for years, you've never cared about the times I come or go. It wasn't until, before the overdose, that you even showed concern. Then, our sex life is boring as hell. You give me three pumps, missionary style and never care about me being satisfied. And you know I'm not satisfied because I tell you."

"That still doesn't mean I allow you to cheat."

"Yes, it does. If you don't care about me being satisfied, sexually, that means you are allowing me to be satisfied elsewhere."

He's shaking his head. "That's not true."

"Let's say I cooked dinner and you came home starving but what I serve you, isn't good or it doesn't fill you up. Sure, you may pick at it and even eat some of it but a little while later, you find yourself in the pantry, looking for a snack. Thomas, I'm not trying to justify my mistakes, but you leave me hungry and you don't care."

"Wow," he says sitting on the end of the bed.

"You say all I'm concerned with is sex when sex is our biggest problem. It's been weeks and technically, the last time doesn't count because I wasn't satisfied."

"Have you gotten it from somewhere else?"

"No but I want too."

"Why haven't you?" he asks.

"Because I promised I would get help. I've held up my end of our agreement, you haven't. And using the excuse of not being able to move pass who I've cheated with, that's a load of crap. You only know I cheated because I told you but even that could be a lie."

"Is it?"

"Look, I'm done with this. Do you want this marriage or not?"

"Yes," he pauses.

"But?"

"Come here," he says holding out his hand. "Please Camille."

I throw the pillow on the bed, walk over and grab his hand. He pulls me into his lap.

"I do love you and I'm sorry for the part I've played in this. Yes, I want our marriage and yes, I want you." He grinds under me. "I'm sorry Camille for it taking me this long to listen to you."

I close my eyes and lean back into him. "And I'm sorry for everything."

He pulls my gown up, rubbing his hand up my chest. "Raise up," he orders.

I do, and he quickly unfastens his pants, kicking out of them. He pulls me back down onto him and I moan.

After a few seconds, he flips me over and stands up to enter me, from behind.

"Yes, um, yes!"

"You like that?" he questions, slapping my butt.

"Yes, give it to me."

"How do you want it?"

"Hard, yea, like that," I tell him.

Thirty minutes later, we're both sprawled on the couch.

"That was amazing," I tell him. "Man, that was good."

"Dang, are you saying I was whack before?"

I don't say anything, instead I get up.

"Camille?"

I laugh. "Not whack but definitely not that. Keep that up and I'm going to get you pregnant."

*****

A few weeks later and Thomas is back to his old

self with these three pumps and a roll. A roll is him rolling off of me, when he's done. It's cool though.

I'm sitting down the street from the house because I'm not ready to go home. I get my phone and open the messenger app.

"Hey, are you busy?" I type, and press send. I tap on the steering wheel and a few seconds later, I get a reply.

"No, I just pulled up to Chicks and Cigars. Care to join me?"

"I would actually but can you wait for me, before you go in?"

"Sure."

"Great, be there in ten."

I pull up and he gets inside my car. I drive to the farthest end of the parking lot and back in.

I look over and he smiles.

"I'm glad you finally reached out."

"Yea well, I had to make sure we wouldn't get caught."

"Shit, it ain't no fun unless there's some risk involved."

"Spoken like a true virgin cheater. Now, stop

talking, push your pants down, to the floor and slide your seat all the way back then lay it down."

"Cam—"

"If you're going to talk, you can get out."

He eyes me but then do what I asked. I raise my dress and maneuver over the console to sit between his legs. I pull a condom out of my bra and tear it open. I cover him and then lick him, once, fully.

"Turn on your side." I direct before turning my back to him, twisting, onto my side and placing one leg on the dashboard. We're laying parallel, in the seat, just enough for him to enter me.

"Aw," I moan, grabbing his thigh. "Just like that."

Twelve minutes later, I'm grabbing some wipes, from the back seat to clean myself up. "Here," I say handing the pack to him.

I look around and when I don't see anyone, I get my panties, from the console and open my door. I quickly slide them on, fix my dress and walk over to the driver's side.

"Thank you," I tell Brock.

"You never have to thank me, for making my night."

"Good, then come on so you can buy me that drink."

Kerri

"Hey babe," I say getting up and giving Mike a kiss when he walks into my office. "I'll be ready in a few minutes."

"What are you working on?" he asks.

"Some new advertising stuff for the windows, fliers and some coupon cards."

"Let me see," he says. I turn the laptop around to him. "That looks good."

"Thanks, I'm getting ready to send it to FedEx Office and then we can head out."

"Kerri, I can never tell you enough how proud I am of you. When I look at all you've accomplished, with this bakery, I am in awe of you."

"Aw, thanks babe."

I finish uploading my designs to the website, close everything out and shut it down.

"Okay, I'm ready." I put the computer into my backpack and grab my purse. I go into the kitchen to make sure everything is off while Mike checks the front.

"Ready?" he asks.

"Yep."

I set the alarm and open the back door. Once I ensure that it's locked, we turn to walk to Michael's car but—

"Sharon," we both say.

"You know her?" I ask Michael.

"Yea but how do you know her?"

"She's married to Adrian but how do you know her?"

"We used to work together," he says.

She laughs. "Is that all?"

I look at Mike.

"What happened to your face?" I ask, concerned.

"Wait, Adrian the guy you had an affair with, is your husband?" Mike asks, looking back to Sharon.

She shrugs.

"Did you know this before we slept together?"

"Why do you think I slept with you, in the first place? Trust me boo, you aren't my type. That bitch was doing my husband, so I decided to do hers."

"Bravo, it's done. Now what?" I ask.

"Now, I want you to keep your filthy hands off my husband."

"What?"

"I know you're still fucking him."

"Girl get off my property. I haven't seen your husband."

"That's a lie. Michael, did you know you married a liar. She was with my husband yesterday and yet; this is who you left me for."

"Lady, there may have been somebody with your husband, yesterday but it wasn't me."

"YOU'RE A LIAR," she screams. "I know it was you."

"Okay, I'm done." I walk over to the passenger side and put my bags in.

"No, you're done when I say we are." She runs to the other side of the car, slamming the door, barely missing my hand.

"It's because of you that I've had to suffer. You think you can have everything but you're a liar. Liar, liar, pants on fire," she begins to sing, taking out a water bottle and flinging a liquid towards me. It gets on my clothes and the car.

"Mike, that's gas."

"What the hell are you doing?" he asks rushing up behind her, grabbing her arms as I dial 911.

"911, what's your emergency?"

"LET ME GO," she's screaming.

"Hello," the operator says.

"Yes, I need police to The Sweetest Things Bakery, 1781 Madison Ave. There's a lady here throwing gas and I'm scared she's going to try to set us on fire."

"You're damn right, bitch. As soon as he lets me go, I'm going to set you ablaze and watch you scream in agony."

"Ma'am, please hurry."

"We have a car in your area that should be pulling up, at any moment."

Seconds later, the police come barreling into the parking lot.

When they finally have her, in handcuffs, we have to wait for the fire department. Although she didn't start a fire, she threw flammable liquids that could still ignite.

I dial Adrian's number.

"Kerri," he answers. "Hey, is everything okay?"

"No, I wish it was, but my husband and I just had a run in with your wife?"

"Oh my God, where?"

"At my bakery."

"Is she still there?" he questions.

"Yes, the police have her because she tried to set me on fire."

"Kerri, I am so sorry, and I can be there in fifteen minutes."

The fire department finally showed up and sprayed off the car. I had to remove all of my clothes. Good thing, I have some in my office.

Walking out, to the car I hear Adrian call my name.

"Kerri, I'm so sorry," he says as Mike walks up.

"Man, you need to keep your problems away from my family," Mike tells him.

"Wait, you're the one Sharon was sleeping with? Wow, I knew your face looked familiar."

"What do you mean?" I ask him.

"She had pictures of him, in her car and it didn't click, until now."

"I didn't know she was your wife, just like I didn't know she was crazy," Mike tells him.

"Regardless of whatever happened before, it's done but why would Sharon think we're still sleeping together?"

"Kerri, Sharon didn't come here for you."

"Then why was she trying to set me on fire?" I ask with confusion.

"To make him suffer," Adrian states, pointing to

Mike. She blames him for the baby she lost."

"Wait, what? Baby?" Mike stutters.

"I guess she never told you. I figured as much but Sharon became pregnant, from the affair. That's the reason she stopped taking her meds.

"Wait," I chuckle, "how long were you two sleeping together?"

"I don't know, maybe a month."

"Three months," Adrian corrects.

"Wow."

"Kerri, I had no idea she was pregnant," Mike protests. "You've got to believe me."

"Adrian, how did Sharon lose the baby?"

"When he broke things off with her and because she wasn't taking her meds, she spiraled. It was bad. One night, she was having a meltdown and left the house. Her car went over an embankment and the impact caused her cervix to rupture."

"Is that what happened to her face?"

"Yeah."

"What does that have to do with me?" Mike asks.

"She was looking for you but you were gone to rehab. After the accident, she was hospitalized and put back on her meds. I thought she was coming around, until a few months ago. I filed for divorce, had to close the coffee shop and now this. She hadn't been home in over a week and before today, I had no idea where she was."

"Wow," I keep repeating.

"Kerri, again I'm sorry for what Sharon did but hopefully, this will be enough for them to keep her hospitalized."

"Thank you, Adrian."

I turn the alarm on, again and lock the door.

"There aren't going to be more women to jump out at us, are they?"

He looks at me as we're getting in the car.

"Kerri—"

"No Mike, I don't want to get into the details of your past affair. We both made mistakes and I never asked you for details and I don't want them now. Is the affair over with?"

"Yes, it was over before I left for rehab."

"Are you having any other affairs?"

"No, I promise."

"Then we move forward."

"All of this happened because of me, so at least allow me to apologize," he requests.

"Go ahead."

"I'm sorry."

"Apology accepted but if any more of your mistakes happen to show up, with love children or trying to set me on fire, things will not end well for you, partner."

"Noted."

Shelby

I walk into The Beauty Shop restaurant, looking around for Derrick. I see him waving his hand.

"Hey," I say, giving him a hug.

"Hey yourself. You're looking good."

"Thanks, so do you."

"I ordered you a sweet tea, extra ice," he tells me.

I smile, "thanks."

"I was happy you finally accepted my invitation to lunch."

"You don't have to say it like I've been dodging you."

"Well," he drags out.

"Whatever," I roll my eyes.

"Are you uncomfortable being here, with me?" he asks with concern.

"To be honest, yes but it has nothing to do with you. I guess, it just feels weird. It's almost like I'm cheating on Brian. I know it sounds crazy."

"No, it sounds like a woman who lost her husband, three months ago."

"I know," I sigh. "It's just weird. Anyway, have you

eaten here before?"

"No, but it looked appealing when I was online seeing what was in this area. I like the Cooper-Young District."

"Me too. The night life is really cool. The girls and I have eaten at Café Ole and Soul Fish, but never here."

"Do you see anything on the menu? If not, I can pay for these drinks and we can go somewhere else."

"I may try, hmm, maybe the BLT."

"Good afternoon, my name is Ronda and I have you a fresh glass of sweet tea. Have you all had a chance to look at the menu?"

"Yes," I reply. "I'll have the B, L, FGT & A with fries and also an order of grill peaches."

"Would you like the peaches to come out first?"

"Yes, please."

"And for you, sir?"

"Um, I'll have the Beastie Boy with fries."

"Sounds good. I'll get that in for you and if you need anything, don't hesitate to flag me down."

"Shelby, it's really good to see you," he says when Ronda walks off.

"You too, Derrick. How are you liking being back home, in Memphis?"

"It's okay. It's nothing like Florida, that's for sure but I needed to come home, for my mom."

"Is she sick?"

"She has stage 3 breast cancer but she's recovering."

"I'm happy that she's recovering but I know it has to be hard, being an only child."

"It can be, but I have a good team of nurses and doctors, ensuring she gets the best care, so it helps. What about you? How have things been, for you?"

"Hectic, these last three months but they're finally settling down. Thank God."

"How is your daughter? Is she sleeping more? Well, I should ask, if both of you are sleeping more."

"Yes, Dr. Cleaves." I reply with sarcasm. "Seriously, we are better. Brian's brother, Brock and his wife, are back in Memphis and I think it helped, having a man around. As for me, I've gotten things squared away with Brian's business and all legal and insurance paperwork done, which was the bulk of what I had to take care of. So, yeah, I've been sleeping better."

Ronda comes back with the grill peaches.

"This smell good," I tell him. "Do you mind if I say grace?"

"Of course not."

"Father, I thank you for the food we are about to eat, remove all impurities so that it is nourishment to our bodies. Bless the hands of the cooks. Amen."

"Amen."

When I look up, he's smiling at me.

"What?"

"You're beautiful."

"Thank you. Now, tell me why you aren't married yet."

"I was waiting on you?"

I roll my eyes. "Will you be for real?"

He laughs. "I don't have the time to date. Between working at the hospital and overseeing my mother's care, I barely have time to eat. Today, was all God's doing and I couldn't be more thankful because I get to enjoy lunch with you."

"Will you stop?" I blush.

"I can't help it. I was dumb for letting you get away."

"Boy, we were sixteen and in high school."

"I know but I should have given you a promise ring or something."

I laugh, putting a slice of peach into my mouth.

"Then when we happened to cross paths, a few

years ago."

"That was a mistake because I was married, and we were going through a rough time."

"And I'd just came out of a relationship with a woman who only wanted the benefits and nothing else. Man, I swore off dating for five years, after her."

"Was she that bad?"

"Worse. She told her parents that I'd proposed marriage. She was so convincing that they even hired a wedding coordinator. I was out of the country, on a mission trip and by the time I came back, they'd paid for everything. Imagine their surprise to find out, we'd only been dating five months."

My mouth has formed into an o.

"Right."

We both laugh as Ronda sits our food in front of us.

"Do you think you'll get married again?" he asks me.

"If God ordains it, I'd love too. What about you?"

"Yes, I'm ready to settle down. I'm so sick of eating hospital and fast food, I can scream. I want a home that has pictures hanging up, of my family, toys strewn about the floor and a wife who's happy to see me come in."

"It'll happen in God's timing. Right now, put your heart in Him and He'll lead you to your wife. In the meantime, on your next off day, I'll cook dinner, for you."

"You will?"

"Sure."

"I'm going to hold you to it so don't be dodging my calls."

"I wouldn't do that."

We finish lunch and an hour later, Derrick is walking me to my car.

"Derrick, thank you for lunch. It really feels good to be out and I meant what I said about dinner."

"I am going to check my schedule tomorrow and I'll let you know a good time."

"Great," I say giving him a hug. "And next time, I let you pick lunch, I don't want no more of this fancy crap."

"Yes ma'am. Drive safe Shelby and text me when you make it home."

I get inside of my car and drive off, feeling conflicted. *Should I have gone to lunch? Is it too early?*

At the red light, a red cardinal sits on the driver's side mirror. When the light changes, he doesn't fly away.

I pull over and let the window down.

"Brian, is this you?" I ask, with tears stinging my eyes.

The bird turns and looks at me and then flies away.

I smile, wiping the tears. Rolling the window up, I put the car in drive and pull off. Raising the volume of the radio, I hear the announcer talking.

"Many times, when death occurs, those left behind go through moments of feeling like their life is on hold. You're conflicted if you laugh, you're conflicted if you go out or you're conflicted for wanting to move on. Is it too soon? Is this the right time? Should I be doing this?

Beloved, you handle your life as you see fit. You taking moments to laugh, love again, have lunch, hang out with friends or whatever doesn't diminish your love for the person who died and neither does it take away your grief. What it means is, you're still alive."

Ray

It's Spring Break and I decided to take the kids on a four-day cruise to the Bahamas. We're docked in Princess Cay and I've been sitting here staring at the pages of this book, 'Hate the Way He Love Me,' by Stacey Covington-Lee.

Although the main character, in her book, is dealing with domestic abuse, this title happens to fit perfectly for the story of my life.

I slam the book closed and lay my head back on the beach chair. I begin to think about how my life was, a year ago. A life of lies. I can imagine, if things hadn't transpired the way they did, Justin and I, probably would've been on vacation as a happy, loving family.

I thank God for pulling back the veil and even though it came with all the chaos of this past year, I'm still grateful. Had God not allowed me to see things, for what they were, I would have still been fighting for a man who only married me because he needed me and not for love.

Man, what a year.

I hear the kids laughing. I look over at them and smile. To watch them now, you wouldn't know all the things we've endured.

Finding out Justin is gay, Cam overdosing, Lyn being attacked and Brian dying … child, I thank God, every day just to have a sound mind. This is why this vacation was needed. I understand more, why Lyn went away to Jamaica.

"Mom," Rashida screams pulling me out of my thoughts, "answer your phone."

"Hello," I answer putting my Bluetooth in.

"Hey, how are you?"

"Hey Anthony, I'm great. What about you?"

"I'm good, still at the office finishing up some things before I pick up Tori, for our flight to Florida."

"Disney World," I laugh.

"Yes," he sighs, "I thought she'd want to go somewhere else this year but as long as she's happy."

"That's all that matters right?" I ask.

"Are you okay? You don't sound good. What's going on?"

"Nothing, just reflecting on this past year."

"Yea, it has been a year. How are the kids? Are they enjoying themselves?"

"Of course. With all this boat has to offer."

"Ray, I was thinking. Since you all are docking in Florida and we'll be there when you get back, tomorrow, why don't you come and join us."

"Anthony—"

"Before you say no, think about it. I'll book an adjoining suite for you and the kids and we can hang out at Disney World and Universal Studios and fly home together."

"Do you think that's a good idea?"

"Ray, Tori loves you. Over the last month, since her mom passed away, you've been there. Your children are older, so I'm sure they understand. Babe, why don't you allow me to do something for you, for a change."

I don't say anything as tears fill my eyes.

"You're always being and doing for everybody else, let me be here for you. No strings attached. Well, not yet."

I laugh.

"Okay."

"Is that a yes."

"Yes Anthony, we will join you in the happiest place on earth."

"Disney World," Rashida says walking up.

I wave her off.

"Send me the information and we'll be there Friday."

"Great, I'll see you then."

"Are we going to Disney World?" Rashida asks, jumping like a five-year-old.

"We're going to Disney World?" JJ asks, his eyes lighting up.

"Calm down," I tell them. "Anthony and Tori are flying into Orlando, tomorrow and he wants us to join them."

"Yes," they all say at the same time.

"Wait, y'all didn't even give me time to finish."

"Mom, we know Mr. Anthony likes you and you like him. Dad has moved on and it's time you do too. We only want you to be happy." Rashida tells me, matter-of-factly.

"As long as he respects you and doesn't make you cry, we won't have a problem," Tristan adds.

"JJ?"

"Mom, if you're happy, I'm happy."

Lyn

I'm at home, getting ready to fix a frozen pizza, when my phone rings. I wipe my hands and slide the bar to answer before putting it on speaker.

"Hello."

"Mrs. Williams, you have a guest downstairs. Paul Williams. Can I let him up?"

I pause.

"Yeah."

A few minutes later, there is a tap on the door.

"Paul, what can I do for you?"

He has a bouquet of flowers and what looks like, food.

"May I come in?"

I step back to let him in.

"These are for you," he says handing me the flowers. "I didn't know if you'd eaten so I bought takeout. Your favorite, Orange Peel Chicken with Vegetable Lo Mein and Crab Wontons."

I roll my eyes and take it from him. Walking over to the kitchen, I motion for him to sit while I grab plates and silverware and put the pizza up.

Neither of us say anything while I take the food out. We both fix our plates and I join him at the kitchen's island. I bow my head and say grace.

After taking a few bites, I look at him.

"What are you doing Paul?"

"First, I wanted to apologize for standing you up, for dinner. It was never my intentions. Second, Kandis is not pregnant by me. I don't know why she said that, but she was lying. She was only there because of PJ."

I continue eating.

"I should have fought harder for you."

I continue eating.

"I was stupid, Lyn and I'm sorry."

I get up and go over to the refrigerator and grab two bottles of water.

"Aren't you going to say something?"

"Say what, Paul? It's been months since everything happened and you're just now showing up. I said everything I needed to, that night. As for fighting for me, yeah, maybe you should have fought harder but that's over and done." I reach for the container and get more chicken and Lo Mein. "I wish I could tell you, the time spent in Jamaica caused me to lose all feelings for you, but I'd be lying. What I did learn, I need to find Lyn again and I can't do that constantly being drug into your mess. You have a new life, live it and leave me out of it."

"I can't do that because I want you."

"No, you don't. You want the comfort of what being with me, gives you. That's because it's all we've ever known. Paul, you chose to be with Kandis, you created a child with her and they are your priority."

"I know, and I made a huge mistake. Lyn, I'm falling apart, without you."

I finish eating and get up to empty my plate. I sit it in the sink. "Paul, I've been gone, for months and you're just now falling apart?"

He gets up and empties his plate. He reaches around me to place it in the sink but doesn't move. I turn to face him. "Paul, why are you really here? Is—"

Before I can finish, he kisses me.

"Whoa, what are you doing?"

"Lyn, I miss you," kiss, "I miss the taste of you," kiss, "I miss the touch of you," kiss, "I need you."

I put my hands on his chest and push him away. He grabs me, by the jaws and kisses me again. This time, it's a kiss like those at the end of the movies, when the guy finally gets the girl.

I relent and give in. We begin pulling at each other's clothes, while we make our way into my bedroom. Fully naked, I lay on the bed and he smiles before joining me.

Sometime later, I keep hearing a vibrating sound. I roll over and when I hit something hard, my eyes pop open. Looking at Paul's back, I realize, it wasn't a dream. The noise goes again.

I nudge him.

"Paul, you need to get your phone."

He huffs before sitting up on the side of the bed. He stands and gets his pants. Pulling out his phone, he scrolls for a second, type something then turns it off.

He gets back under the covers and pulls me into him.

The next morning, I get up to the smell of coffee. I stretch before going into the bathroom to shower and dress. Walking into the kitchen, Paul is in his boxers, singing.

"Uh, good morning."

"Good morning, love. How did you sleep?"

"I actually slept, for the first time, in a while but we need to talk."

"Uh oh," he says.

"Last night shouldn't have happened."

"Lyn, there's nothing wrong with a man, making love to his wife. Look, I know things are complicated with us, but I love you and I'm going to fight for you, this time."

"I don't want that. Paul, while I enjoyed last night, it doesn't change a thing between us. We're still getting a divorce."

"Is this because of Kandis? Baby, we aren't together."

"You may not be, but she is the mother of your son and a constant reminder."

"Of what?"

"Of brokenness. Come on Paul, you know that girl is not going to freely give you up and I don't have time to constantly fight with somebody over what should be mine. I don't have the energy."

"I understand and right now, I'm going to enjoy breakfast with my wife, then I'm going to get dressed and go home but I will not stop fighting to get you to love me again."

*****

For the past two months, Paul and I have been

Netflix and chilling. I haven't told anybody, other than Cam because I didn't want them to make a big deal out of it. No, I haven't decided to get back with him but I'm enjoying the time we've been spending, together.

I had a doctor's appointment today, for a physical, near Paul's office so I decided to stop by.

"Hey Mrs. Williams, it's so good to see you."

"Hey Annie, is Paul in?"

"Yes ma'am, he's finishing up a meeting in the conference room. You can wait in his office and I'll let him know that you're here."

I go in and sit on the couch. I must have dozed off because Paul is shaking me.

"Hey," he smiles, "you must have stayed up all night."

I yawn, "no thanks to you."

He laughs.

"Where are you coming from?"

"A doctor appointment. I stopped by to see if you wanted to do lunch."

"Um," he says scrolling on his iPad, "I can do that, but I'll need about ten minutes."

"I'll be right here."

He walks out, and I sit back on the couch and grab

my phone to play a game. A few minutes later, Kandis comes in.

"Paul, did you happen to see my ring when you left the house this morning because—" she stops when she realizes I'm sitting here. "Oh, hey."

"Kandis, I didn't know you were still working here?"

"I don't but I stop in, from time to time," she tells me.

"Why is that?"

"To see my fiancé."

"Oh, your fiancé, as in Paul?"

"Who else?"

"Who else," I repeat. "How long have you two been engaged?"

"He asked me on Valentine's Day."

"Are you sure or is this another one of your lies, like that fake pregnancy?"

"Fake pregnancy?" she pulls her shirt back to display a baby pump. "There's nothing fake about this."

"Wow," I stand up, "well, congratulations."

"Wait, who told you my pregnancy was a lie?"

Paul walks through the door. He stops when he sees both of us, standing there.

"Congratulations on the engagement and your two

new babies." I tell Paul.

"Two?" Kandis asks, shocked, "no sweetie, I'm only pregnant with one."

"So am I," I say dropping the ultrasound on the table and walking out.

Chapter 9

Renewal

"As we stand, tonight, under the moon and stars that God created, we join in communion with Michael and Kerri as they renew their commitment of love for and to each other. We know that no marriage is perfect but that's because God allows us to work for the things we desire.

Marriage, takes work but if every day was easy, how could you appreciate the times, it wasn't. God allows struggle, not as punishment but the harder the struggle, the sweeter the snuggle. You, as husband and wife, have to commit to working hard for your marriage.

This is why, I ask that as you continue in this union, you vow to be all in. We sometimes think, we only have to give fifty percent of ourselves to make one hundred, but what are you doing with the other half of you?

Here's what you do.

Give yourself away and let God be your guide. You do this by letting love, for one another be stronger than anger. Compromise when it's easy and let wisdom speak, when it's not. When there's a misunderstanding, resolve it and don't allow it to build. If you need help, ask for it. If you're mad, tell each other. And don't bring anything from your past, into your current. Most of all, keep outside folk, out of your marriage.

Do you each make that vow, to one another?"

"We do."

"Michael and Kerri, do you continue to choose, each other as your spouse, forsaking all others, promising to love and cherish, to honor and endure, in sickness and in health, in poverty and in wealth, in the good that may lighten your ways and especially when bad may darken your days. Do you vow to be true to each other in all these things until death shall part the two of you?"

"We do."

"May I have the rings? With the new rings, they are an outward symbol of love made by two people. The true symbol of love is what you hold in your heart. These rings, symbolizes, to others, the vow you've made but what matters is what your actions prove; to one another. These rings signify a wedding took place, but your actions prove a marriage, ordained by God."

She places the rings in our hands.

"As you place the rings on the finger, repeat after me. With this ring, I commit to forgiving you for the past—"

"With this ring, I commit to forgiving you for the past," we repeat.

"And starting over, brand new."

"And starting over, brand new."

"This ring is a symbol of our new beginning."

"This ring is a symbol of our new beginning."

"And will serve as a sign of our continued happiness and joy."

"And will serve as a sign of our continued happiness and joy."

"Dear God, thank you for the recommitment of Michael and Kerri. God, I ask that you accept this renewal and bless it with your power. Give them wisdom to know that what you've join together, they shall not allow man, woman, neither child or foe put asunder. We thank you for the union and by your grace, may it always be blessed. Amen.

Ladies and gentlemen, I present to you Mr. and Mrs. Michael and Kerri Davis."

"Pastor Reeves, thank you for coming all this way to do this for us," I say giving her a hug after we sealed the renewal with a kiss.

"You know I wouldn't have missed this, especially in this beautiful place."

"Okay everybody," Shelby says getting our attention, "before the party officially begins. I've planned something special, for all of us."

A few employees of the resort come out and begins to pass out the white lanterns and lighters, I'd purchased earlier.

I look around at everybody.

Kerri, Mike and MJ.

Raylan, Anthony, Rashida, JJ, Tristan and Tori.

Chloe, Todd and Tamah.

Pastor Reeves, Mama Denise, Taya and her husband Trent.

Lyn and Kelsey.

Camille, Thomas, TJ and Courtney whose holding Brinae.

"Tonight, is about renewal and as I thought about that, I realized we could all stand to renew our lives. One definition of renewal means the replacing or repair of something that is worn out, run-down, or broken.

I don't know about y'all but after the year we've

had, it left us worn out, run-down and broken. So, I purchased these lanterns and it just so happens that we're in Maui, which means, fire of God. With these lanterns, I'd like for each of us, to have our own, personal, renewal ceremony.

As you're lighting your lantern, think of the things that may have worn you out or broken you, this past year, month, week or lifetime. As you think about it, let the fire, from the lighters, be a symbol of God's fire and allow it to burn away anything that seeks to cause us brokenness.

I've asked Pastor Reeves or Mama Denise to pray, as we watch the lanterns float away."

Mama Denise steps forward.

"Dear God, as we stand watching these lanterns float away, we ask that you carry with it, anything that causes us to be weighed down. God, we ask you, tonight, to release the weight of rejection, loss, anger, bitterness, resentment and pain. As you release it, fill us up with hope, joy, favor, patience, love and understanding.

God, as we stand, in the midst of family and friends; who all endured this past year, we thank you for recovery and restoration. Father, some have recovered relationships, others recovered joy, some recovered their peace of mind and all have recovered you. Thank you, God.

Thank you for the return of your children. Thank you that the pain, didn't provoke us to anger. Thank you for not allowing us to succumb to our flesh. Thank you, God that although there has been broken hearts, promises, trust, some late-night toiling, some early morning tears and some pain; you've allowed us to make it here.

Not just anywhere, but to a place whose name means fire of God. Thank you, father. Thank you for not allowing us to give up. Thank you for not allowing our fears and scars, to hold us back. Thank you for the recovery, the restoration and the renewal. In your name, we pray, amen."

"Amen," we collectively say.

"To being family, to loving each of you, to the many blessings to come, to the laughter and the tears, to new life, to new beginnings and to all that is to come. I love each of you until death do us part!" Ray states.

"Now, let's party."

Thank you all so much for the support of When the Vows Break. The love shown has blown my mind. THANK YOU!!

As this series comes to a close, I intentionally left Camille and Lyn's story hanging because their lives will play out, in the next series Ms. Nice Nasty. As of now, that series is definitely not Christian Fiction, however, you never know how God will lead.

Who knows, maybe God will lead me to give each of the leading characters, in this series, their own storyline, one day. I don't know but I hope you'll continue on the journey, with me.

Be on the lookout for Ms. Nice Nasty in September 2019.

Until then, pick up another book by me and Happy Reading.

Lakisha

About the Author

 Lakisha Johnson, native Memphian and author of over fifteen titles was born to write. She'll tell you, "Writing didn't find me, it's was engraved in my spirit during creation." Along with being an author, she is an ordained minister, co-pastor, wife, mother and the product of a large family.

She is a blogger at kishasdailydevotional.com and social media poster where she utilizes her gifts to encourage others to tap into their God given talents. She won't claim to be the best at what she does nor does she have all the answers; she is simply grateful to be used by God.

Again, I thank you for taking the time to read my work! I cannot express what it means to me every time you support me! If this is your first time reading my work, please check out the many other books available by visiting my Amazon Page.

For upcoming contests and give-a-ways, I invite you to like my Facebook page, AuthorLakisha, follow my blog https://authorlakishajohnson.com/ or join my reading group Twins Write 2.

Or you can connect with me on Social Media.

Twitter: _kishajohnson | Instagram: kishajohnson | Snapchat: Authorlakisha

Email: authorlakisha@gmail.com

Also available

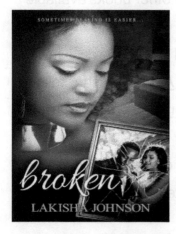

Broken

Gwendolyn was 13 when her dad shattered her heart, leaving her broken. Her mother told her, a daddy can break a girl's heart before any man has a chance and she was right. Through many failed relationships and giving herself to any man who showed interest, she knew she had to get herself together. So, she gave up on men.

Until Jacque. He came into her life with promises to love, honor and cherish her; forsaking all others until death do they part. Twelve years later, he has made good on his promises until he didn't.

https://www.amazon.com/dp/B07QZCW9ZX

The Family that Lies:
Forsaken by Grayce, Saved by Merci

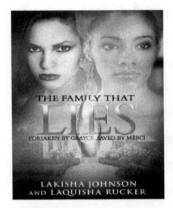

Born only months apart, Merci and Grayce Alexander were as close as sisters could get. With a father who thought the world of them, life was good. Until one day everything changed.

While Grayce got love and attention, Merci got all the hell, forcing her to leave home. She never looks back, putting the past behind her until … her sister shows up over a decade later begging for help, bringing all of the forgotten past with her. Merci wasn't the least bit prepared for what was about to happen next.

Merci realizes, she's been a part of something much bigger than she'd ever imagined. Yea, every family has their secrets, hidden truths and ties but Merci had no idea she'd been born into the family that lies.

https://www.amazon.com/dp/B01MAZD49X

The Family that Lies: Merci Restored

In The Family that Lies: Merci Restored, we revisit the Alexanders to see how life has treated them. Three years ago, Merci realized she'd been a part of something much bigger than she ever could have imagined. Sure, every family has their secrets, hidden truths and ties but Merci had no idea she'd been born into the family that lies ... without caring who it hurts!

Now, years later, Merci finds herself in the midst of grief, a new baby and marriage while still learning how to pick up the broken pieces of her life.

All while Melvin is still raising hell!

In this special edition of The Family that Lies, there will be questions answered and new drama but I have to warn you ... there will also be tragedy, hurt and of course LIES!

https://www.amazon.com/dp/B07P6LGQQ6

The Pastor's Admin

DISCLAIMER This is Christian FICTION which includes some sex scenes and language. ***

Daphne 'Dee' Gary used to love being an admin ... until Joseph Thornton. She has been his administrative assistant for ten years and each year, she has to decide whether it will be his secrets or her sanity. And the choice is beginning to take a toil.

Joseph is the founder and pastor of Assembly of God Christian Center and he is, hell, there are so many words Daphne can use to describe him, but none are good. He does things without thinking of the consequence because he knows Dee will be there to bail him out. Truth is, she has too because ... it's her job, right? A job she has been questioning lately.

Daphne knows life can be hard and flesh will sometimes win but when she has to choose between HIS SECRETS or HER SANITY, this time, will she remain The Pastor's Admin?

https://www.amazon.com/dp/B07B9V4981

The Marriage Bed

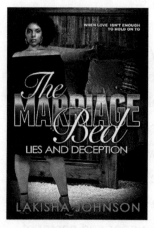 Lynn and Jerome Watson have been together since meeting in the halls of Booker T. Washington High School, in 1993. Twenty-five years, a house, business and three children later they are on the heels of their 18th wedding anniversary and Lynn's 40th birthday. Her only request ... a night of fun, at home, with her husband and maybe a few toys.

Lynn thinks their marriage bed is suffering and wants to spice it up. Jerome, on the other hand, thinks Lynn is overreacting. His thoughts, if it ain't broke, don't break it trying to fix it. Then something happens that shakes up the Watson household and secrets are revealed but the biggest secret, Jerome has, and his lips are sealed.

Bible says in Hebrews 13:4, "Let marriage be held in honor among all, and let the marriage bed be undefiled, for God will judge the sexually immoral and adulterous." But what happens when life starts throwing daggers, lies, turns and twists?

https://www.amazon.com/dp/B07H51VS45

Still Fighting: My sister's fight with Trigeminal Neuralgia

What would you do if you woke up one morning with pain doctors couldn't diagnose, medicine couldn't minimize, sleep couldn't stop and kept getting worse?

What would you do if this pain took everything from your ability to eat, sleep, wash your face, brush your teeth, feel the wind, enjoy the outdoors or even work? What would you do if this pain even tried to take your life but couldn't shake your faith?

Still Fighting is an inside look into my sister's continued fight with Trigeminal Neuralgia, a condition known as the Suicide Disease because of the lives it has taken. In this book, I take you on a journey of recognition, route and restoration from my point of view; a sister who would stop at nothing to help her twin sister/best friend fight to live.

It is my prayer you will be blessed by my sister's will to fight and survive.

https://www.amazon.com/dp/B07MJHF6NL

The Forgotten Wife

All Rylee wants is her husband's attention.

She used to be the apple of Todd's eye but no matter what she did, lately, he was just too busy to notice her.

She could not help but wonder why.

Then one day, an unexpected email, subject line: Forgotten Wife and little did she know, it was about to play a major part in her life.

They say first comes love then comes ... a kidnapping, attacks, lies and affairs. Someone is out for blood but who, what, when and why?

Secrets are revealed and Rylee fears for her life, when all she ever wanted was not to be The Forgotten Wife.

https://www.amazon.com/gp/product/B07DRQ8NPR

Other Available Titles

A Compilation of Christian Stories: Box Set

Dear God: Hear My Prayer

2:32 AM: Losing My Faith in God

When the Vows Break 1

When the Vows Break 2

Bible Chicks: Book 2

Doses of Devotion

You Only Live Once: Youth Devotional

HERoine Addict – Women's Journal

Be A Fighter - Journal

CPSIA information can be obtained
at www.ICGtesting.com
Printed in the USA
LVHW051308020919
629654LV00016B/1645